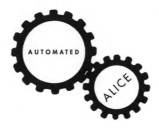

AUTOMATED ALICE

Also by
Jeff Noon

Vurt
Pollen

AUTOMATED

ALICE

JEFF

NOON

ILLUSTRATIONS BY

HARRY TRUMBORE

Crown Trade

New York

Copyright 1996 by JEFF NOON
ILLUSTRATIONS COPYRIGHT
© 1996 BY HARRY TRUMBORE

Published by Crown Publishers, Inc., 201 East 50th Street, New York, New York 10022. Member of the Crown Publishing Group.

CROWN is a trademark of Crown Publishers, Inc.

Design by Alexander Knowlton @ BEST Design Incorporated

Random House, Inc. New York, Toronto, London, Sydney, Auckland http://www.randomhouse.com/

Printed in the United States of America

Library of Congress Cataloging-in-Publication Data
Noon, Jeff
    Automated Alice/Jeff Noon.—1st ed.
    Sequel to: Alice's Adventures in
        Wonderland/Lewis Carroll.
    I. Carroll, Lewis, 1832–1898. Alice's
    adventures in Wonderland. II. Title.
PR6064.045A96   1996
823'.914—dc20   96-24822

ISBN 0-517-70490-0

10 9 8 7 6 5 4 3 2 1

1ST EDITION

Now in my trembling days I seek
All comfort to be found
In contemplation of the past;
When we rowed aground
At Godstow on the Thames' bank,
With my sweet Alice bound.

And there beneath a spreading elm
I told a tale of joy
To a child who smiled to hear
This older man's employ.
But now that girl is married to
Some fine and dashing boy.

And I am near my maker's house,
There to sup the chalice,
With one last tale to tell as time
Works my shape with malice;
Of how a child will become my
Automated Alice.

Now in these final days I seek
To find a future clime;
In which my Alice can escape
The radishes of time.
Faster, faster ticks the clock that
Turns to end this rhyme.

AUTOMATED

ALICE

THROUGH

THE CLOCK'S

WORKINGS

ALICE was beginning to feel very drowsy from having nothing to do.

How strange it was that doing absolutely *nothing at all* could make one feel so tired. She slumped down even deeper into her armchair. Alice was visiting her Great Aunt Ermintrude's house in Didsbury, Manchester; a frightful city in the North of England which was full of rain and smoke and noise and big factories making Heaven-knows-what. "I wonder how you *do* make Heaven-knows-what?" thought Alice to herself, "perhaps they get the recipe from somebody who's only recently died?"

The thought of that made Alice shiver so much that she clutched at her doll ever so tightly! Her Great Aunt was a very strict old lady and she had given Alice this doll as a present with the words, "Alice, the doll looks just like you when you're in a tantrum." Alice thought that the doll looked *nothing* like her at all, despite the fact that her Great Aunt had sewn it an exact (if rather smaller) replica of Alice's favourite pinafore, the splendidly warm and red one she was currently wearing. Alice called the doll Celia, not really knowing the reason for her choice. Alice would often do things without knowing why, and this made her Great Aunt very angry indeed. "Alice, my dear," she would pronounce, "can't you make sense for once?"

Alice now hugged the Celia Doll even closer to her chest, where she wrapped it in the folds of her pinafore: this was all because of the lightning that was flashing madly outside the window, and the November rain that was falling onto the glass, sounding very much like the pattering of a thousand horses' hooves. Her Great Aunt's house was directly opposite a large, sprawling cemetery, which Alice thought a horrible place to live.

But the very worst thing about Manchester was the fact that it was—Oh dear!—*always* raining. "Oh Celia!" Alice sighed to her doll, "if only Great Uncle Mortimer was here to play with us!" Great Uncle Mortimer was a funny little man who would always have a treat tucked away for Alice: he would amuse her with jokes and magical tricks and the magnificently-long words that he would teach her. Great Uncle Mortimer was, according to her Great Aunt, "big in the city," whatever that could mean. "Well," said Alice to the doll, "he may well be *big* in the city, but when he gets back to his home he's really rather small. Perhaps he's got two sizes, one for each occasion. How splendid that must be!" Great Uncle Mortimer would spend every night smoking on his pipe whilst adding up huge rows of numbers, and wolfing down a great plateful of the radishes that he grew for himself in the vegetable garden. Alice had never seen so many numbers before (or so many radishes). She was not awfully good at mathematics (or radish eating), and the numbers one to ten seemed quite adequate to her. After all, she only had ten fingers. Why should anybody need more than ten fingers? (Or, for that matter, more than one radish?)

These idle thoughts only made Alice realise how dreadfully bored she was. Great Aunt Ermintrude had three daughters of her own (triplets in fact) but they were all much older than

Alice (and Alice always had trouble telling them apart) so they weren't much fun at all! There was nothing to *do* in Manchester. The only sounds she could hear were the *pitter-pattering* of the rain against the window and the *tick-tocking, tick-tocking* of the grandfather clock in the corner of the room. The housemaid had dusted the clock this very morning and the door of it was still open. Alice could see the brass pendulum swinging back and forth, back and forth. It made her feel quite, quite sleepy, but at the same time quite, quite restless. It was at this very moment that she noticed a solitary white ant marching across the breakfast table towards a sticky dollop of Ecklethorpe's Radish Jam; the maid had neglected to remove this in her cleaning. Alice had tried a spoonful of the radish jam (it was Uncle Mortimer's favourite preserve) on a piece of toast that very morning but had found the taste of it too sick-ly sour. The ant was now running over the jigsaw puzzle that Alice had spent the whole morning trying to complete, only to find (frustratingly) that fully twelve pieces were missing from the segmented picture of London Zoo. "Oh, Mister Ant," Alice said aloud (although how she could possibly tell it was a Mister from that distance is quite beyond understanding), "how is it that you've got *so* much to do, whilst I, a very grown-up young girl, have got so very little to do?"

The white ant, of course, did not bother to make an answer.

Instead it was Whippoorwill who spoke to Alice. "Who is it that smiles at ten to two," he squawked, "and frowns at twenty past seven, every single day?" Whippoorwill was a green-and-yellow-plumed parrot with a bright orange beak who lived in a brass cage. He was a very talkative parrot and this pleased Alice—at least she had somebody to converse with. The trouble was, Whippoorwill could only speak in riddles.

"I don't know," answered Alice, grateful for the diversion. "Who *does* smile at ten to two, and frowns at twenty past seven, every single day?"

"I'll tell you the answer if you open my cage."

"You know I daren't do that, Whippoorwill. Great Aunt would be very angry."

"Then you'll never know," squoked the parrot. (Squoking is how a parrot talks, exactly halfway between speaking and squawking.)

"Oh well," Alice thought, "I suppose it won't do very much harm to open the cage door just a little way." And even before the thought had finished itself, Alice had pulled herself and Celia Doll out of the armchair and made her way over to where Whippoorwill's cage stood on an alabaster stand. "Now you really won't try to escape, will you?" said Alice to the parrot, but the parrot had no answer to give her: he clung to his perch and turned a quizzical eye towards the young girl. Seeing that quizzical eye Alice could do nothing more than to release the tiny brass catch and let the cage door swing open.

Oh dear! Whippoorwill immediately flew out of his cage; his bright feathers made a fan of colours and his screechy voice seemed to fill the room. "Whatever shall I do now?" cried Alice, aloud. "My Great Aunt shall have to have *words* with me!" The parrot flew all around the room and Alice tried her best to catch hold of his tail feathers, but all to no avail. Finally he flew directly into the grandfather clock's open casing. Alice quickly ran to the clock; she slammed the door shut, trapping the poor parrot inside. The door had a window in it and Alice could see Whippoorwill making a fearful commotion trying to escape. "Now let *that* be a lesson to you, Whippoorwill," said Alice. She looked up at the clock's face and saw that it was almost ten to two in the afternoon. At precisely two o'clock each day her Great Aunt would come calling for Alice to take her afternoon writing lesson: Alice could not possibly be late for that engagement. (She had not at all bothered to complete yesterday's assignment on the correct use of the ellipsis in formal essays: the truth be known, Alice didn't even know what an ellipsis was, except that it was made out of three little dots, just like this one is . . .) Despite the young girl's predicament, the two hands of the clock seemed to put a smile on its moon-like face: it was then that Alice found the answer to Whippoorwill's latest riddle, but when she looked through the glass window into the casing all she could see was the blur of the parrot's wings as he flew upwards into the clock's workings.

Whippoorwill vanished!

Alice looked here and there for the parrot, but finding only a single green-and-yellow feather floating down, she decided that she must go into the clock's insides herself. Alice therefore opened up the door and climbed inside. It really was a very tight squeeze inside the clock, especially when the pendulum swung towards her. "That pendulum wants to cut my head off," thought Alice, and then she looked up into the workings to discover where the parrot had got to. "Whippoorwill?"

she cried, "where on the earth are you?" But there was no trace of the parrot at all! Alice climbed aboard the pendulum as it swung past her, and then started to climb up it, which is quite a difficult task when you have a porcelain doll called Celia in your hands. But very soon she had reached the top of the pendulum and now her head was pushing against the very workings of the clock, and the *tick-tocking, tick-tocking* seemed very loud indeed! And that naughty Whippoorwill was still nowhere to be seen.

Just then Alice heard her Great Aunt's stentorian voice calling over the clock's tickings: "Alice! Come quickly, girl!" the voice boomed. "It's time for your lesson, dear. I do hope you've done your assignment correctly!"

"Oh dear, oh dear, oh dear!" cried Alice, "whatever shall I do? Great Aunt is early for my lesson! I really must find Whippoorwill. He must be around here somewhere!" And so Alice climbed up the pendulum even further until, with a sudden ellipsis . . .

. . . Alice *vanished!*

Now I don't know if *you* have ever vanished, but if you have, you will know it can be quite a fearsome experience. The strangest thing was this: Alice knew that she had vanished, but, even so, she could still see herself! Imagine that; you know that you've vanished, but you can still see yourself! So then, how is it that you know that you've vanished?

But Alice was far too busy to pay much attention to these

thoughts: she was presently rushing down—at an ever-increasing
pace!—a long tunnel of numbers. The numbers flashed by her
eyes like shooting stars in the night, and each number seemed to
be larger than the last one. They started out from one-thousand-
eight-hundred-and-sixty (which was the number of the present
year) and rapidly increased until Alice could no longer see where
the count was taking her. Why, to count this far, one would need
a million fingers! Ahead of her she could see Whippoorwill flying through the cascade of numbers, until what looked like a
very large and a very angry one-thousand-nine-hundred-and-
ninety-eight clamped his numbersome jaws around the ever-so-
naughty bird. Alice plummeted forwards (if you can plummet
forwards, that is) until she felt herself being eaten up by that very
same number.

   Down, down, down. Through an endless tubing Alice fell.
"Whatever shall we do, Celia?" she said to the doll she still
clutched in her fingers; and she wasn't all *that* surprised when
the doll answered, "We must keep on falling, Alice, until we
reach the number's stomach." "I didn't even know that numbers *had* stomachs," thought Alice. "Great Uncle Mortimer will
be most astounded when I tell him this news." When suddenly, *thump! thump! thump!* down Alice came upon a heap of
earth, and the fall was over.

⚙⚙⚙

Alice was not a bit hurt: the earth was quite soft, and she
jumped up in a moment. She looked around only to find herself standing in a long corridor under the ground. The walls

and the floor and the ceiling of the tunnel were made of dirt, and it curved away in both directions until Alice felt quite funny trying to decide which way to go. "Oh Whippoorwill," she cried, "wherever have you flown to?" And then she heard three men approaching around the corridor's bend. She knew it was three men because she could hear six footsteps making a dreadful noise. But what should come around the corner but a rather large white ant! He was quite the same size as Alice and he had on a tartan waistcoat and a pair of velvet trousers. (Although I suppose you can't really have a *pair* of six-legged trousers: you can have a sextet of trousers—but that sounds too much like a very strange musical composition.) Dangling between the ant's antennae was an open newspaper which completely obscured his face, and from behind which he could be heard muttering to himself.

"Tut, tut, tut! How dare they? Why, that's disgusting! Tut, tut, tut!" The newspaper was called *News of the Mound* and if Alice had managed a look at the newspaper's date she would have received a nasty shock, but all her attention was focused on the headline, which read: TERMITES FOUND ON THE MOON! Alice was so puzzled by this news, and the ant was so engrossed in his reading, that they both banged into each other!

"Who in the earth are you?" the ant grumbled, folding up his paper and looking rather surprised to find Alice standing there.

"I'm Alice," replied Alice, politely.

"You're a *lis*?" the ant said. "What in the earth is a lis?"

"I'm not a *lis*. My name is Alice." Alice spelt her name: "A-L-I-C-E."

"You're a lice!" the ant cried. "We don't want no lice in this mound!"

"I'm not a lice, I'm Alice! I'm a girl."

"Are you now? Then I suppose this might very well be yours?" Upon which utterance the ant produced a tiny piece of crooked wood from his waistcoat pocket. "I found it lying in the tunnel, just a few moments ago."

"Why, yes it does belong to me," cried Alice. "It's a missing piece from my jigsaw!"

"Well take it then, and in future may I ask you to refrain from cluttering up the tunnels with your litter."

"I'm very sorry," replied Alice, taking the jigsaw piece from the ant's grasp. It showed the picture of a single white ant crawling up the stem of a flower. "I shall place this in London Zoo, just as soon as I get back home." And she slipped the jigsaw piece into her pinafore pocket.

"But it's only a picture," sniffed the ant, "not a living creature."

"That's quite all right," Alice replied, "because he's going to live inside a picture of London Zoo. Is that today's newspaper?"

"I sincerely hope it's today's paper! I've just paid three grubs for it."

"But it says that termites have been found on the Moon?"

"So?"

"But nobody's been to the Moon!"

"What are you going on about?" the ant demanded. "The humans have been travelling to the Moon for years now! For years, I tell you! What, exactly, are you doing in this mound?"

"I'm looking for my parrot."

"A parrot, you say? This wouldn't be a green-and-yellow parrot, with a big orange beak, who just can't stop asking riddles?"

"Yes, that's Whippoorwill! Where did he go?"

"The parrot, he went that-a-way," said the ant, pointing back down the corridor with one of his antennae.

"Oh thank you, Mister Ant. You've been ever so helpful."

"How dare you, young miss!" exclaimed the ant, raising himself onto his back legs and blocking her path. "You have made not one, but two factual errors: firstly, I am not an *ant*. I am a termite."

"Oh I am sorry," said Alice. "But surely there's not that much difference between ants and termites?"

"Stupid child! Just because we've both got six legs and two sections, and just because we both live in highly organised societies comprising winged males, wingless females and winged Queens, you presume ants and termites to be all but identical. You couldn't be more wrong, dear girl. Why, there's a thousand differences between us!"

"Please tell me one," asked Alice.

"Tell you one what?"

"A difference between a termite and an ant."

"Well, now . . . let me think . . . I'm sure there was something . . . it's in here somewhere . . ." The termite was tapping his head with one of his antennae as he pondered. "Of course! We termites are vegetarians, while the horrible ants are carnivores. In fact . . ." and here the termite looked around rather nervously as he whispered to Alice, "ants like to eat termites for breakfast. On toast! I suspect that the ants are jealous because *they* haven't been found on the Moon. Quite a mound of difference, I think you'll agree?"

Alice *did* agree, but she wasn't sure why. "What is your name, Mister Termite?" she asked.

But this latest (very polite) question only made the termite even angrier: his antennae fairly bristled with indignation. "And *that*," he trumpeted, "brings me to your second mistake, for, if you had been paying attention to my previous statement, you would have recognised that I am completely wingless and therefore, logically, I am a female termite."

"Very well," said Alice, getting just a little exasperated herself now, "what is your name, Mrs Termite?"

"Mrs? Mrs? Do I look like a Mrs? Only the Queen is a Mrs! I told you already that the Queen has wings. What is the matter with you?"

"Oh!" cried Alice, "*Miss* Termite, you're just too . . . too . . . too logical for me!"

"Logical? Of course I'm logical. I'm a computermite."

"Whatever's a computermite?"

"Exactly what it sounds like, silly. I'm a termite that computes. I work out the answers to questions. Now, what is *your* question?"

"Very well," began Alice, trying her best to keep her anger in check. "What is your name, Miss Computermite?"

"Name?" squeaked the termite. "Names, names, names! What would I know about names? I'm a termite, for digging's sake! Termites don't have names! Whatever next? You'll be asking if we've got bicycles in a minute!"

Just then, Alice heard a trundling noise coming from behind her, and when she turned to look, what should appear around the corner but a male termite, on a bicycle! It was quite an ordinary bicycle except that it had two sets of pedals (rather like a tandem) which the male termite pedalled at furiously with his middle and his hind legs, whilst clinging to the

handlebars with his forelegs. (This is one of the few cases when
two plus two plus fore equals six.) Alice knew it was a male termite because of the wings on his back, and she felt rather
proud to have worked out this piece of logic; although why he
wasn't flying through the tunnel rather than bicycling through
it was quite another question. However, the male termite never
gave her a chance to ask this question because he was obviously in a terrible hurry; he simply pedalled past Alice and the
female termite at a terrific speed, shouting at them as he did
so, "Come on, you two, hop to it! The Queen of the Mound
has received a question from Captain Ramshackle and we must
answer it immediately. Chop chop!" And with that he disappeared around the curve in the tunnel.

Alice was quite taken aback by this whirlwind appearance.
"Who on earth is Captain Ramshackle?" she asked of Miss
Computermite, but the female termite was already hurrying
along the tunnel after the bicycle. "Come on then," the termite shouted back at her, "there's no time for questions, we've
got a question to answer!" Alice thought that sentence completely illogical. "Oh dear, Celia," she said to her doll, "we shall
never be home in time for our writing lesson now." And it
wasn't until after she'd finished the sentence that Alice
realised she no longer had Celia in her hands. "Oh bother!"
she said to herself. "Not only have I lost Whippoorwill, I've also
lost Celia. And not only that, I've also lost myself! Great Aunt
Ermintrude is going to be very, very angry."

And with that Alice started to run along the corridor after
Miss Computermite.

THE   WRIGGLING

OF   A   WORM

HUNDREDS,

indeed thousands, of other termites joined with Alice in her race to find Whippoorwill. Of course these termites weren't really after the parrot at all: they were after the answer to the question that Captain Ramshackle had posed to the Queen of the Mound. Eventually Alice managed to catch up with Miss Computermite, and immediately she asked of her this question: "What is the question that you're trying to answer?"

"Oh, it's a tricky one, indeed," Miss Computermite answered while still running along the corridor at an alarming pace. "Captain Ramshackle wants to know which number, when multiplied by itself, will give the answer minus one. And that question doesn't *have* an answer!"

"But that doesn't seem such a difficult question," said Alice.

"Well, as you must surely know," the termite replied, "one times one is one, and minus one times minus one is also one, because two negatives always make a plus."

"Do they?"

"They do indeed."

"But I was taught that two wrongs do not make a right."

"That's true in real life. In computermatics, however, it's quite the opposite." And with that Miss Computermite put on an extra dash of speed.

Alice felt quite breathless from trying to keep up because she had only two legs whilst the termite had six: the only possible way she could keep up (because six divided by two equals three) was by running *three* times as fast as she was used to. But keep up she did. "So then," said Alice, running, "if I had two milk bottles on a table, and I took one of them away, and then I took the other away, I would then be left with one milk bottle. Is that what you're saying?"

"I'm not saying that at all," replied the termite, running. "I'm saying that if you took one milk bottle away from a table, and then another milk bottle away from a table, and then if you multiplied all the milk bottles that were left on the table together, you would get another milk bottle."

"That doesn't make sense, but it sounds like an excellent way to get free milk."

"Exactly! Captain Ramshackle is hoping to get a free bottle of milk, and more power to his elbow."

"He's going to drink the milk with his elbow?"

"Of course not," laughed Miss Computermite. "You're really rather stupid for a *girl.*"

"And you're really rather large for a *termite,*" said Alice.

"*Au contraire,*" replied the termite (in French), "you're really rather *small* for a girl." And as she listened to this answer, millions, indeed trillions of other termites thundered past Alice (some of them on bicycles) until Alice thought that she was caught up in a gigantic wave of termite frenzy.

"How on earth do you answer the questions?" Alice asked, still running.

"Well," Miss Computermite began, also still running, "it's all based on the beanery system."

"Whatever's that?"

"Well, a bean is either here, or it's not here. Don't you agree?"

"I agree entirely," replied the running Alice.

"So then, logically, if a bean is here it counts as one bean, and if it isn't here, it counts as a not bean. And from this knowledge, when the beans are arranged in patterns, it is possible to spell out many the question and many the answer. Why, with only a mere octet of beans (or not beans) one can spell out all of the numbers and all of the letters of the alphabet. And quite a few punctuation marks as well! So then, imagine a trillion beans! What problems you could work out with a trillion beans! And the same principle applies to termites of course: a termite is either here, or it isn't here. And we termites are even better than beans at being here or not being here because we've got legs, and therefore we can move much faster than beans."

"What about jumping beans?" asked Alice.

"Don't talk to me about jumping beans," replied the termite, angrily.

"So, this Captain Ramshackle asks the Queen a question, and all you termites answer it."

"That's correct."

"Where does Captain Ramshackle live?" shouted Alice, loudly. (She had to shout this question out loudly, because the noise of six times a trillion termite legs, all of them running, can make a fearsome thundering.)

"Captain Ramshackle," began the termite, mysteriously, "lives *outside the mound.*" She said these last three words very mysteriously indeed. In fact, she said them *mysteriously* mysteriously.

Alice was rather excited by this news. "Does that mean," she shouted, "that *I* can get outside of the mound?" Alice was excited because she was almost certain that Whippoorwill had found his way out of the termite mound by now.

"Why, that's exactly where you're going," answered Miss Computermite, "because this is how we tell Captain Ramshackle the answers to his questions: we march out from the mound so that the Captain can study our formation and, by studying our formation, by noting which termites are here and which are not here, the Captain can find out the solution to his latest question."

"But I thought you said that this latest question didn't have an answer?"

"It doesn't, and that's why I'm scurrying around even more than is usual. I'll tell you one thing though . . ."

"And what's that?" shouted Alice, grateful to know that Miss Computermite was only going to tell her *one* thing: Alice had learned more than enough *things* already that afternoon.

"Why, only that you're a *part* of the answer, Alice: otherwise, why are you running so very quickly?"

"And what happens after you've answered the Captain's question?"

"We all march back into the mound again, of course, carrying the next question."

But Alice had no intention of marching back into the mound: once she was out, she was staying out. "Maybe I shall be home in time for my writing lesson," she said to herself. Which gave her an idea. "Miss Computermite," she said out loud, "you're awfully good at answering questions, aren't you?"

"I most certainly am. Fire away, young girl."

"Answer me this then: what is the correct usage of an ellipsis?"

"No, no . . . don't tell me . . . let me think . . ." the computermite pondered, "I know it . . . I'm sure that I do . . . now let me just . . . there . . . I have it!"

"Yes?" urged Alice excitedly.

"The correct usage of an ellipsis . . ." the computermite

announced grandly, "is for the removal of greenfly from a rose bush."

"I beg your pardon?"

"An ellipsis . . . it's a kind of gardening implement . . . isn't it?"

"Oh, this is no good at all!" spluttered Alice. "My Great Aunt will be furious!"

This statement stopped Miss Computermite completely in her tracks. "You've got a great *ant*?" she asked, astonished.

"I most certainly have. Her name is Ermintrude."

"The great ant has got a name?!"

"Yes she has, and very, very strict she is too."

"Upon my mound!" squeaked the termite in a frightened voice.

"What's wrong, Miss Computermite?" asked Alice. "You look quite scared."

"Just keep your great ant Ermintrude away from me!" the termite pronounced, and then off she set at an even faster pace than before.

"I wonder what's bothering Miss Computermite?" pondered Alice. "Did I say something wrong?" And then she set off after the termite, doing her utmost to catch up.

Presently Alice did catch up, and just as she did so, she saw a faint light glowing from a distant hole in the mound. The trillions, even zillions of termites, they were all scurrying forwards into the light and Alice was quite caught up in their rush: she *was* a part of the answer.

And then, quite suddenly, Alice was wriggling like a worm in a pair of giant tweezers as she was carried upwards into the sky. Up, up, up. How dizzy Alice felt! "My, my!" cried a faraway voice. "What have we here? I do believe I've got a wurm in my computermite mound!" The voice said the word *worm* with a U inside it, and Alice could hear the U inside the word *wurm* as it was said. "How splendid!" the voice cried. Alice couldn't see where the voice was coming from, and she didn't really care to, because right about then Alice was dropped from the tweezers so that she landed on a sheet of glass. The sheet of glass was quickly slid under another piece of glass which looked very much like a glass eye. Alice was squashed flat! "Now then," said the voice, "let us see what we have captured. Magnification: five and ten and fiftyfold!"

Alice realised then that she was being looked at, rather closely, and she tried to think about what had a glass eye that allowed somebody to look at you rather too closely. "I'm being looked at through a microscope!" was her answer. She had seen her Great Uncle Mortimer use a microscope in his study: he used it to examine his numbers and his radishes.

"My, my!" the faraway voice stated. "We seem to be looking at a tiny *girl*, a minuscule *girl*, an ever-so-small *girl*. What's *she* doing in my computermite mound? What a very splendidly random occurrence!"

Alice looked up the glass eye of the microscope and saw another eye—a giant eye—an almost human eye—looking back down at her. "Oh, if only I could travel up this microscope," thought Alice, "then I could become my real size again." But after all, she *had* already that afternoon climbed up the pendulum of a clock and vanished and shrunk, so this shouldn't be too difficult a task for her: And so it proved. Alice felt herself passing through the glass eye of the microscope and then through another glass eye, and then through yet another glass eye, and yet another, and then finally a final glass eye, and by this time she felt quite faint! In fact, Alice fainted quite away!

$$\infty \bigcirc$$

The third thing that Alice knew upon awakening was that she was lying on an extremely uncomfortable camp-bed with a horsehair blanket placed over her. The second thing Alice knew was that she was surrounded by a jumbling of tumbling objects and items. And the *first* thing she knew was that an old and rather untidy badger was leaning over her with a cup of tea in his hand, from which he was trying to make her drink. Alice did drink, because she felt quite weak from her travels, but the tea tasted dark and she told the old badger so. "I'm afraid the tea *is* dark," the badger agreed, "but that's only because it's got no milk in it. You see, I'm desperately short of money at the present moment, and I was trying to invent a free bottle of milk, but my computermites couldn't work out the solution to that little problem, I'm afraid: it made them go into a dreadful tizzy. Still, perhaps if I lighten your tea with a little fish juice . . ." The badger proceeded then to squeeze a live goldfish over Alice's cup of tea.

This made Alice spring to her feet. "Please don't harm that poor fish!" she called out.

"But he *likes* flavouring tea," the badger answered, waving the fish under Alice's nose. "This a Japanese tea-flavouring fish."

Alice politely declined the taking of fish juice and then asked of the badger, "Are you Captain Ramshackle, by any chance?"

"I am indeed by chance the one and only Captain of Ramshackle," the badger agreed, bowing at the waist. As he bowed, a cloud of talcum powder rose upwards from his thick, black-and-white-streaked hair. "And what is your name?"

"My name is Alice."

"You're a girl, aren't you, Alice?"

"Of course!"

"A *human* girl?"

"And what is wrong with that?" Alice asked, having noticed that the badger was actually a mixture of a man and a badger.

"Nothing . . . it's just that . . . well . . ." pontificated the badgerman, "and after all . . . there aren't *that* many . . . that is to say . . . if I may be so impolite . . . there aren't many . . . well, it's just that there aren't many human girls around these days."

"Why ever not?" asked Alice, rather worried by this news.

"Oh murder!" screamed Captain Ramshackle, all of a sudden. "Whatever am I to do now? Murder, murder, murder! The Jigsaw Murder!"

"Whatever's the matter?" asked Alice, quite alarmed at the outburst.

"There's been a spidercide and the Civil Serpents are trying to put the blame for it on me." The badgerman threw his paws into the air with this statement. "I didn't have an alibi, you see?" (Alice wasn't sure what a *spider's side* had to do with anything; and she imagined that Ali Bi must be some relative, a cousin say, of Ali Baba, the poor woodcutter in the Arabian fable who discovered the magic words "open sesame," which allowed him to enter the cave of treasures. But if this was true, she couldn't for the life of her work out why a badger should need the relative of an Arabian woodcutter in order to prove his innocence. And anyway, shouldn't he have said Ali Bibi?) "I fear that the Civil Serpents will soon arrest me," the badger was now saying. "Oh, troubleness! And all because of a certain piece missing from a silly jigsaw."

Alice was curious at hearing this news, mainly because she had tried and failed to complete a jigsaw that very same morning. (If it was still that very same morning, of course.) "What do you mean by a Jigsaw Murder?" she asked.

"May I welcome you, Alice, to my humble abode," the badgerman replied, calming himself and totally ignoring Alice's question. Alice greeted the badgerman in return, took a little sup from her unlightened cup, and then looked around the room she had found herself in: Captain Ramshackle's humble abode was suffering from extreme untidiness. It was crammed to the walls with what the Captain called his "miscellaneous objects": rocking-horses and blow-pipes, frogs' legs and battering rams, blotting paper and tiger feathers and garishly coloured maps of countries called Epiglottis and Urethra, a seven-and-a-half-stringed guitar and a deflated cricket ball (Alice couldn't work out how you could possibly deflate a cricket ball!), a tear-stained mirror and a nosebrush and a stuffed Indian Lobster and a tumult of other things that Alice could make neither head nor tail of. (Especially the deflated cricket ball, because, of course, a deflated cricket ball has neither a head nor a tail.) And Captain Ramshackle was no tidier than his room was: in fact he was worse. The old badgerman was dressed in a patchwork suit of many different clothes and his hair was night-black with a streak of silver riding down his brow.

"I see that you're admiring my suit, Alice," the Badger Captain said, moving over to a mound of earth that rested on a leather-topped desk. "It's quite splendidly chaotic, isn't it? Of course, it cost me not a penny, because I made this suit myself out of a book of tailor's samples. One must make one's ends meet, when one is a Randomologist."

"And what is a Randomologist?" asked Alice.

"What else could it be but somebody who studies Randomology?" replied Captain Ramshackle.

"And what is Randomology?"

"What else could it be than what a Randomologist studies?"

Alice felt that she was getting nowhere at all with her questions so she decided to ask no more. Instead she walked over to the desk where Captain Ramshackle was fiddling about with the mound of earth. Alice could see numerously numerous termites running hither and thither over the soil. "What I want to know," Ramshackle asked, "is what in the earth were you, a young *girl*, doing in my computermite mound?"

"I was trying to get out," replied Alice.

"And very glad I am that you managed it. Of course, every home's got one these days: computermite mounds are most useful for the solving of problems. I dug this one up myself, you know, only yesterday, in a radish patch."

"A radish patch?" said Alice.

"What's so strange about that? Termites are vegetarians, you know?"

"I know."

"My previous mound was getting rather antsy, you see. Anyway, I'd heard on the badgervine that a rather nice Queen had moved her troops into an old radish patch in Didsbury—"

"Didsbury!"

"Yes. Do you know it?"

"I was there only a few minutes ago."

"Well, you must have very fast feet then, because it's five miles from here."

"Oh dear," said a very confused Alice.

"However, this is only a portable mound." Alice tried her very best to imagine a badger carrying a mound of earth through the streets, but no matter how hard she tried, she still couldn't imagine it. "They say that if you could get enough computermites into a big enough mound," the badgerman continued, "you would have a termite brain equal in imagination to the human mind. But, according to my miscalculations, that would make the—"

"Don't you mean calculations," interrupted Alice.

"I thought I had already told you that I was a Randomologist?" replied the badgerman, crossly. "Now what would a Randomologist be doing making calculations? No, no; a Randomologist makes miscalculations, and according to my miscalculations, a computermite mound with the imagination-power of a single human would be as large as the whole world itself! But what I want to know, Alice, is this: how in the earth did you manage to get inside the mound?"

"I just found myself there," Alice said, quite dizzy from the Captain's miscalculations. "Could you tell me the time, please?"

"I most certainly can," replied Ramshackle, rolling up his left shirt sleeve to reveal a tiny clock fastened around his wrist. "It's seven minutes past five."

"Oh goodness. I have completely missed my afternoon writing lesson!"

"No you haven't: it's seven minutes past five in the morning."

"In the morning?!"

"That's right. I do all my best miscalculations during the early hours. Maybe it's a breakfast writing lesson that you've missed? I know that most young creatures these days learn how to read from studying the labels on jamjars."

"But what day is it today?" Alice asked.

Captain Ramshackle rolled up his right shirt sleeve where a second wrist-clock was fastened. "It's a Thursday," he announced.

"A Thursday! It should be a Sunday."

"It should always be a Sunday but, unfortunately, it hardly ever is."

"What month is it?" asked Alice.

Ramshackle rolled up his right trouser leg. Another tiny clock was fastened to his ankle. "It's a bleak twenty-fourth of November in shivery Manchester."

"At least that's right!"

"Of course it's right: this is a right-leg watch, after all!"

"And what year is it, please?" Alice then asked, quite confused.

Ramshackle consulted yet another tiny clock, strapped to his left ankle this time. "It's 1998, of course."

"1998!" cried Alice. "Oh dear, I am ever so very late for my lesson. I set out in 1860, and I still haven't reached the writing table yet. Whatever shall I do?"

"You say that you left Didsbury village in 1860? Why that's . . . that's . . . why I don't know how long ago that is. Do you?" Alice tried to work it out, but she couldn't. "No matter," said Captain Ramshackle, "I'll ask the mound how long ago it is." And with that he picked up his pair of tweezers and proceeded to pluck a number of termites from the earth: he rearranged them here and there and then set them on their way back into the mound. "The answer should be arriving in a few minutes," he said. And then he started to consult something lying on his desk beside the computermite mound.

"Oh this is very confusing," cried Alice, edging even closer to the desk in order to see what Captain Ramshackle was looking at.

"Confusing? Splendid!" the Captain cried, not even looking up from his task.

"It's not at all splendid. It's extremely confusing."

"Confusing *is* splendid."

"Is that a jigsaw you're doing?" asked Alice, having finally dared to look over his shoulder.

"No it is not," fumed the Captain. "This is a jigglesaurus."

"What's the difference?"

"A jigsaw is a modern creature that finally makes sense,

whilst a jigglesaurus is a primitive creature that finally makes nonsense."

"None of the pieces seem to fit at all," said Alice. "There's no picture there."

"Exactly so. Everything adds up to nothing. You see, I'm a Randomologist: I believe the world is constructed out of chaos. I study the strange connections that make the world work. Did you know that the fluttering of a wurm's wings in South America can bring about a horse-crash in England?"

"No, I didn't know that," said Alice, "in fact I don't even know what a horse-crash *is,* but I *do* know that a worm doesn't have wings."

"Doesn't it?" Ramshackle replied. "How on the earth then does it fly?"

"A worm doesn't fly. A worm wriggles."

"Does it? Excellent! Even better. The wriggling of a wurm in South America causes a horse-crash in England. Oh chaos, chaos! Splendid chaos! Now what's this doing here?" Ramshackle had plucked a jigsaw piece up from his desk with the aid of his tweezers. "This little piece seems to fit perfectly in place!" he cried out loud. "We can't have that! Indeed, no." He slipped the jigsaw piece under his microscope. "It's a section of a badger's head I believe."

"That belongs in *my* jigsaw," said Alice.

"Splendid! And here was I fearing that my jigglesaurus was starting to make sense, of all things." Alice took the offending piece from Ramshackle and then placed it in her pinafore pocket. "You know, I thought *you* were a wurm, Alice," the Captain continued, "when first I saw you marching out of the mound."

"I'm not a worm," answered Alice.

"I didn't say you were a worm, Alice. I said you were a *wurm*."

"Why do you keep saying the word with a U in the middle of it?"

"Because it stands for *Wisdom-Undoing-Randomised-Mechanism*. Don't you see, Alice? The world is totally random and all the Civil Serpents who try to find out the rules of it are just squeezing at strawberry jelly."

Finally, Alice got round to asking the Captain what a Civil Serpent was.

"Those tightly knotted buffoons!" grunted the badgerman in reply. "The Civil Serpents are these hideous snakes that writhe around all day in the Town Hall, making up all these petty laws against nature. Nature, of course, follows her own laws, and these are the laws of Randomology, as worked out by yours truly. The Civil Serpents regard me as a trouble-maker, as though *I* make the trouble! No, no: the Universe makes the trouble; I'm just the watcher of the trouble. And this is why they're claiming the good Captain Ramshackle is guilty of the Jigsaw Murder."

"Has somebody been murdering jigsaws?"

"Silly, silly, silly! It's a murder by jigsaw. Not by jigglesaurus, mind. I mean, what interest have I in jigsaws? Those perfectly logical, slotting-together pictures? No indeed, jigsaws bore me to tears. Oh, those slithering oafs! *Civil!* I'll give those serpents *civil!* And they're claiming that I killed the spiderboy. Spidercide? Me? How could I possibly . . . why I love spiders!"

At this moment Captain Ramshackle looked over to a (quite

fearsomely large!) stuffed and mounted example of the arachnid species that rested amongst his miscellaneous objects.
"Well, never you mind the details, Alice. Suffice it to say that I,
the Captain of Ramshackle, am totally incapable of such a
crime. Oh, I feel so ostracised!"

"You feel so ostrich-sized?" asked Alice.

"Not at all!" cried Ramshackle. "It's the serpents who have
buried their heads in the sand, not me. Surely *you* must see,
Alice, that I couldn't possibly kill a spider?"

Alice accepted that fact quite easily, having witnessed the
badgerman's bristling indignation at such close quarters, not
to mention the fresh cloud of talcum that billowed loose from
his hair. (Oh dear, I just said I wasn't going to mention the
cloud of talcum powder, only to find that I already have men-
tioned it. I must be getting rather tired in my old age, Alice. In
fact, I do believe that I will take to my bed now, because it is
getting rather late, and this is quite enough writing for one
day. I will see you in the morning, dear sweet girl . . .)

Zzzzzzzzzzzzzżzzzzzzzzzzzzzzzzzz

(There, that's better. Now then, where was I?)

Oh yes; Alice tried her best to calm Captain Ramshackle
down by asking for an explanation of what, exactly, a wurm
(with a U in it) was.

"The science of Randomology," the Captain began, clearly
relieved to have the subject changed, "states that a wurm is a
parasite who likes to make a stolen home in a computermite

mound. Once settled there the wurm does its very
make the termites give the wrong answers. The Civil Serpents,
of course, think that wurms are a pest to the orderly system:
they try to *kill* the wurms. But I, Captain Ramshackle, inventor
of Randomology, would like to *invite* the wurms into my
mound. And you know something, Alice . . . ?" And here the
Captain looked around from side to side nervously and then
bowed his head close to Alice's ear in order to whisper: "Some
people actually *eat* the wurms."

"Eat worms!" Alice exclaimed, quite forgetting the incorrect
spelling.

"Wurms, Alice. W . . . *u* . . . r . . . m . . . s! Some people eat them."

"But that's . . . that's . . . that's disgusting! Whatever for?!"

"It makes you go crazy, of course."

"But why would you want to go crazy? Why that's . . . that's
crazy!"

"Exactly so, Alice! Knowledge through nonsense. That's my
motto. I welcome the wrong answers! Would you like to hear a
song I've written about it? It's called 'Trouser Cup.'"

"Don't you mean trouser cuff?"

"What in the randomness is a Trouser Cuff?"

"Isn't it a kind of trouser turnup—"

"A Trouser Turnip!" bellowed the Captain. "There's no such
vegetable!"

"But there's also no such thing as a Trouser Cup," protested
Alice.

"Exactly!" cried the Captain, upon which he commenced to
make a funny little dance and to sing in a very untidy voice:

"Oh spoons may dangle from a cow
With laughter ten feet tall;
But all I want to know is how
It makes no sense at all.

Oh shirts may sing to books who pout
In rather rigid lines;
But all I want to turn about
Is how the world unwinds. "

Captain Ramshackle then knocked over a pile of his miscellaneous objects (one of which included a croquet mallet,
which fell onto the shell of the Indian Lobster, cracking it
open). "That looks like a very crushed Asian Lobster," Alice
stated.

"That Lobster is indeed a crustacean!" the badgerman
replied, before continuing with his song:

"It makes no sense at all you see,
This world it makes no sense.
And all of those who disagree
Are really rather dense.

Oh dogs may crumble to the soap
That jitters in the dark;
But all I want to envelop
Is how it makes no mark.

> *Oh fish may spade and grow too late*
> *The trousers in the cup;*
> *But all I want to aggravate*
> *Is how the world adds up.*
>
> *It's got no sum at all you see,*
> *This life has got no sum.*
> *And all of those who disagree*
> *Are really rather dumb."*

The Captain broke off from singing and turned back to the computermite mound. "Ah ha!" he cried. "Here's your answer!" He had placed his eye against the microscope. "Oh dear . . ."

"What is it?" asked Alice.

"Young girl," he said, "you are one hundred and thirty-eight years late for your two o'clock writing lesson. You need to talk to Professor Gladys Chrowdingler."

"Who's she?"

"Chrowdingler is studying the Mysteries of Time. Chrownotransductionology, she calls it. Only Chrowdingler can help you now. Don't you realise, Alice? You've actually travelled through time!"

"I'm just trying to find my lost parrot," Alice replied.

"I saw a green-and-yellow parrot flying out of the microscope, some two-and-a-feather minutes before you did."

"That's him!" Alice cried. "That's Whippoorwill. Where did he go to?"

"He flew out of that window there." Ramshackle pointed to a window that opened onto a garden. "He flew into the knot garden . . ."

"I don't care if it is a garden, or not a garden," said Alice, quite missing the point. "I simply must find my Great Aunt's parrot!" And with that she climbed up onto the windowsill and then jumped down into the garden. The garden was very large and filled with lots of hedges and trees, all of which were sprinkled with moon dust. And there, sitting on the branch of a tree some way off, was Whippoorwill himself!

"Be careful out there, Alice," shouted Ramshackle through the window. "Times may have changed since your day."

But Alice paid that badger no mind, no mind at all, so quickly was she running off in pursuit of her lost parrot.

ALICE'S

TWIN TWISTER

ALICE

was glad to be aboveground and out-of-doors at last, even if she was rushing madly around in rectangles through the garden's pathways. "This garden is so complicated!" she exclaimed to herself. Again and again she scampered down long, gloomy corridors lined with hedgerows and around tight corners only to bump—at the end of each breathless journey—against yet another solid wall of greenery. "This *is* a garden, this is *not* a garden," she repeated to herself endlessly as she ran along: Alice couldn't get Captain Ramshackle's description of the garden out of her head. "And if this really is a not garden," she told herself, "well then I really shouldn't be here at all! Because I most definitely am a young girl. I'm not *not* a young girl." All these tangled thoughts made Alice's head spin with confusion. It reminded her of Miss Computermite's description of the beanery system. "A garden, like a bean," Alice thought, "is either here, or it's not here. And this garden is most definitely here! Even if it is terribly gloomy and frightening." Putting her fear aside (in a little red pocket inside her head which she kept for just such a purpose), Alice sped on and on through the morning's darkness, around more and more corners.

Every so often she would come upon small clearings, in each of which a gruesome statue would be waiting, silent and still in the ghostly moonlight. These statues weren't anything at all

like the statues that Alice had seen in the few art galleries that
she had visited. For one thing they weren't carved from stone;
rather they were made out of bits and pieces of this and that,
all glued together higgledy-piggledy; shoes and suitcases and
coins and spectacles and curtains and books and hooks and
jamjars and tiny velvet gloves and horses' hooves and a thousand other discarded objects. And for another thing—unlike
the works in the art galleries—these garden statues didn't
seem to want to portray real people at all; rather they looked
like *monstrous, perverted images* of the subject, especially in this
spectral light and with the rustling of dying leaves all around.
"What strange portraits you have in 1998," Alice announced to
a statue that looked a little bit like her Great Aunt Ermintrude
and even more like a sewing-machine having a fight with a
thermometer and a stuffed walrus. And then she was off and
running once again.

"I'm sure I'm only going around in squares and circles,"
cried Alice, presently. "The trouble is—I think I'm totally lost
now." Alice pondered for a moment on what being partially
lost might be like, but could come up with no better answer
than that it would be like being only partially found. "And I
wouldn't like *that* at all," she whispered, shivering at the
thought of it. "Now, where in the garden has Whippoorwill got
to? Why, only a few minutes ago I could see him clearly sitting
in his tree: now I can't see anything at all other than these tall
hedges and all these corners and corridors in the darkness and
all these funny statues. And I don't even know how to get back
to Captain Ramshackle's house any more! I shall be forever

lost at this rate, never mind totally! This garden is more like a maze than a garden." And then it came to her: "This garden *is* a maze!" she cried aloud. "It's a *knot* garden. Not a *not* garden. That's what Captain Ramshackle meant. Oh how silly of me! The word has a K in it, rather than an empty space. All I have to do now is work out which knot the garden is tied up in. Then I can untie it and find out where Whippoorwill is perched."

The trouble was, Alice knew of only two knots: the bow and the reef. Her Great Uncle Mortimer had demonstrated a double sheepshank knot to her only the previous evening, but she had found it much too difficult to follow each end of the rope in their up-and-under and in-and-out travels. "And anyway," Alice had thought at the time, "whatever is the use of a knot that tied two sheep together by the legs?" (Alice knew that the shank was somewhere on the leg, although she wasn't quite sure whereabouts exactly.) "I shall never find Whippoorwill," Alice thought now, whilst running along a particularly convoluted pathway of hedgerows, "if this knot garden turns out to be a double sheepshank garden!"

Just at that moment who should appear over the top of the nearest hedge but Whippoorwill himself! He gathered his wings about him, landed, and then squawked out the following riddle: "What kind of creature is it, Alice, that sounds just like you?"

"Oh, Whippoorwill!" cried Alice. "Wherever have you been? You know that I'm not very good at riddles. Is it *me* that sounds like me? Is that the answer?"

"Poor Alice! Wrong Alice!" squawked Whippoorwill. "Another clue for poor, wrong Alice: this creature has got your name, only wrongly spelt."

"Oh I understand now, Whippoorwill," said Alice, remembering a misunderstanding she had once had with a certain Miss Computermite. "At last I've worked out one of your riddles! The answer is a lice, which is a kind of insect, I think."

"Explain your answer, girl."

"Well, your question, Whippoorwill, was this: 'What kind of creature is it that sounds just like you?' Now then, the two words *a lice* sound just like my name, Alice, only wrongly spelt, because they've got a space between the a and the lice." She said this quite triumphantly, and Whippoorwill glared angrily for a few moments (during which Alice really did believe she had stumbled across the correct answer) before flapping his wings gleefully and pronouncing: "Wrong answer, Alice! Wrong answer!" *Squawk, squawk, squawk!* "Try again, silly girl."

This made Alice very angry indeed. "Why don't you just stop this nonsense right this minute, Whippoorwill," she said in a firm voice, "and fly back home with me to Great Aunt Ermintrude's?"

But the parrot only flapped his green-and-yellow wings at Alice and then flew off from the top of the hedge. He vanished into the knotted maze of the garden. Alice tried her very best to run after the beating of his wings, but all around her the stark branches tried to clutch at her pinafore and the Autumn leaves under her feet seemed to crackle like dry voices. Here and there amidst the leaves Alice noticed various worktools—

hammers, screwdrivers, chisels, even a pair of compasses—that were littering each pathway. "Somebody's being very untidy in their work," Alice said to herself whilst running. "My Great Aunt would certainly punish me severely for leaving my pencils and books in such disarray in her radish garden. But never mind such thoughts, I must try to capture Whippoorwill." So Alice kept on twisting and turning along the alleyways of the garden's maze until she found herself even more lost than she had been before.

"Oh dear," sighed Alice to herself, flopping down against the nearest hedge (and nearly cutting her knees on a discarded hacksaw lying in the grass), "I'm ever so tired. Maybe if I took just a little nap, I would then be more refreshed for this adventure . . ."

But just as Alice was dozing off, she heard somebody in a rather croaky voice calling out her name. "Alice?" the croaky voice called, "is that you hiding there behind the hedgerow?"

"This is indeed Alice," replied Alice, sleepily, "but I'm not hiding; I'm only trying to find my parrot."

"You're looking in quite the wrong place," croaked the voice.

"And who are you?" Alice asked, rather impatiently.

"Why, I'm you of course," the voice answered.

"But that's impossible," replied Alice, full of indignation, "because *I'm* me."

"That leaves only one possibility," said the voice: "I must be you as well."

The funny thing was, the voice from the garden certainly *did* sound like Alice's voice, if rather croaky, and very confused

Alice was upon hearing it: "How can I be in two places at one time?" she pondered. "But then again and after all," she added to herself, "I am in *two* times at one place, 1860 *and* 1998, so maybe this isn't all that very strange." Alice then pulled herself together (as best you can in a knot garden) and asked the voice this question: "Where in the knottings are you, croaky voice?"

"I'm right behind you, Alice," the voice replied, croaking-ly, "at the very centre of the maze, which lies just behind the hedgerow you are resting against. I have your parrot here with me."

"Oh thank you for catching him! But how can I find you?" Alice asked.

"Why, I'm only some few feet away from you, behind this very hedgerow."

"But you know very well, Miss mysterious voice, that this is a knot garden: I could be miles and miles away from you along all the twistings and the turnings."

"You could always *cut* your way through, Alice."

This made Alice pay proper attention: she would never have thought of such an idea on her own. She turned around to peer through the branches but they were too thickly interwoven: Alice could see only sparkles of colour through the gaps. "Haven't you a penknife?" the voice asked.

"I most certainly have not!" cried Alice in exasperation; and then (after a second's further pondering) she added, "But I've got something even betterer, even sharperer!" (In her excitement Alice had forgotten all about her grammar.)

○⚙○

A longer than long time later (because the branches were very thick and the hacksaw was more blunt than sharp) Alice finally managed to cut her way through the hedgerow. It was almost daylight by the time that she had pushed aside the final branches: and there she found herself at last, in the very centre of the maze. The statue of a young girl was standing upon a podium inside a circle of trees and shadows. She looked a lot like Alice, that statue, especially with the early morning's sunlight sheening her face; the statue even wore a (rather stiff-looking, granted) replica of Alice's red pinafore. Alice was quite taken aback by the resemblance. Why, for a whole second, Alice didn't know which girl she truly was! But on the statue's left shoulder Whippoorwill the parrot was perched. And stretched between the statue's outstretched hands was a long and writhing and very angry-looking, purple-and-turquoise-banded snake!

"Oh dear," cried Alice (in a whisper), "I do hope that snake isn't poisonous!"

"Not only is this snake poisonous," replied the statue in the croaky voice that Alice had heard previously, "it is also extremely venomous."

"Is there a difference," Alice asked (not even pausing to think about how a statue could speak), "between poisonous and venomous?"

"Most certainly there is: anything can be poisonous but only a snake can be venomous. Venom is the name of the poisonous fluid secreted from a snake's glands. The origins of the word can be traced back to the goddess Venus, thereby implying that snake venom can be used as a love potion. Perhaps it was this usage that directed Queen Cleopatra of Egypt to use this particular snake as her instrument of suicide. After all, this is an *asp* that I hold in my hands, also known as the *Egyptian cobra.*"

"Why ever don't you throw the snake away?" asked Alice of the statue.

"How can I?" the statue replied. "I can't even move. After all, I am a statue."

"But you can talk, so you must be a very special statue," said Alice.

"I *am* a very special statue. My name is Celia."

"But that's my doll's name!" Alice cried (having quite forgotten, once again, until that very moment, that her doll was still missing).

"Yes, that's me," the statue croaked to Alice, "I'm your doll."

"You're Celia?"

"Yes, that's my name."

"But you're much too large to be my doll," exclaimed Alice. Indeed, the statue was exactly the same size as Alice.

"I'm your twin twister," the statue said.

"But I haven't got a twin sister," replied Alice, quite mishearing.

"I didn't say twin sister, I said twin twister. You see, Alice, when you named me Celia, all you did was twist the letters of your own name around into a new spelling. I'm your anagrammed sister."

"Oh goodness!" said Alice, "I didn't realise I'd done that. How clever of me." And then Alice finally worked out Whippoorwill's last riddle; she realised that the statue-doll sounded just like her in the way she spoke, and their names were the same, only misspelt: Celia and Alice.

"The trouble with you, Alice," croaked Celia, "is that you don't realise you've done anything, until it's much, much too late. Whereas *I*, your twin twister, I know exactly what I've done, even before I've done it."

"Who turned you into this garden statue, Celia?"

"Pablo the sculptor."

"And who is this Pablo?"

"Presently I shall tell you. For the moment, however, I'm quite helpless unless you remove this snake from my fingers."

"Who put the snake in your fingers?" asked Alice.

"The Civil Serpents of course. Who else? They don't want us statues moving around freely, that would break all the rules of reality."

"But—"

"Alice, there's no time for further questions. Kindly remove this asp from my grasp."

"However shall I remove that snake," Alice asked herself, "without getting myself poisoned? Or, indeed, venomed? Oh well, I suppose I can only try my very best if I'm ever going to get us all back home in time for my writing lesson. Now, what was it that Great Uncle Mortimer had said about dealing with dangerous creatures? Look them in the eye, that was it: look them in the eye and recite the Lord's Prayer."

So Alice did look the snake in the eye: only, just as she was about to start her rendition of the Lord's Prayer the snake *hissed!* at her. Alice was sure she could hear certain words in between each hiss. They sounded something like this: "Do you mind, young lady? I'm an Under Assistant of the Civil Serpents!" And so very fearful a noise the snake made that Alice cleanly forgot *every single word of the Lord's Prayer.*

"Now look here, Mister Snake," she cried (having decided that the snake was male for some reason), "I do believe that you're not very civil at all, keeping my doll under lock and fang." But the snake just carried on hissing and wriggling and writhing and slithering and flickering out his forking tongue and showing off his fine set of fangs. It was then (whilst looking deep into the snake's jaws) that Alice noticed a tiny piece of wood that was speared onto the left-side fang. "I wonder if that's another of my missing jigsaw pieces?" Alice said to herself. "I simply must retrieve it, but how can I when the Lord's Prayer has quite simply vanished from my mind?" She racked her brains to remember the words, but the only "prayer" she could now recite all the way through was the lullaby called "Go to Sleep, Little Bear." The reason she could remember this poem so well had a lot to do with the fact that it had only four lines containing only twenty-two words, many of which were repeated:

> *"Go to sleep, little bear.*
> *Do not peep, little bear.*
> *And when you wake, little bear,*
> *I will be there, little bear."*

So this was the "Lord's Prayer" that Alice recited to the
Under Assistant of the Civil Serpents whilst at the same time
fixing her gaze, icily, upon his. Only, for this rendition, Alice
(quite against her will) changed the words slightly:

> *"Go to sleep, little creep.*
> *Do not peep, little creep.*
> *And when you're deep, little creep,*
> *I will not weep, little creep."*

Alice felt despondent at losing the rhyme between *there* and
bear in her new version of the lullaby, but ever so pleased at
having replaced it with the new rhymes between *sleep* and *peep*
and *creep* and *deep* and *weep*. She thought her creation a much
better poem! Not that the Under Assistant paid much mind to
the ins and outs of poetic rhyming schemes; he was altogether
too very tired to care anymore. His head slumped into slum-
ber. Snakes don't have eyelids of course, but if that snake had
had them, he would have closed them then. When Mister
Snake was quite asleep, Alice removed (very carefully) the jigsaw piece from his left fang. It showed only a pattern of
purple-and-turquoise scales but Alice knew that it would fit
perfectly into the reptile house section of her jigsaw picture of
London Zoo. She popped it into her pocket (alongside the
badger piece and the termite piece) and then unwound (also
very carefully) Mister Snake from Celia's fingers. Alice then
carried the snake over to the nearest hedgerow where she
placed him gently down in a bundle of leaves. Mister Snake

wrapped himself into a reef knot and then into a bow, and finally into a double snakeshank, in which convoluted shape he started to loudly snore.

"Alice, you have released me from servitude!" With that croakment the statue stepped down from her podium with a creaking gait, which sounded very much like a creaking gate. Celia came up very close to Alice and, once there, she shook Alice's hand.

Alice felt very shivery to be shaking a porcelain hand, but shake it she did. "Celia," she cried, "I'm very pleased to have found you and Whippoorwill once again, but how in the garden did you get to be so tall for a doll?"

"I'm not a doll anymore," replied Celia, "I'm a terbot."

"A turbot!" exclaimed Alice. "That's a kind of fish, isn't it?"

"Indeed it is: a European flatfish with a pale-brown speckled one-dimensional body. But that definition only counts when the word's got a U in it."

"Oh, I'm dreadfully sick of words with U's in them rather than their proper letters!"

"A terbot, on the other hand, is an automated creature powered by termites."

"Termites?"

"Exactly so, Alice. Termites. I have termites in my brain. Take a look." Celia bent forwards at her squeaking waist and then turned a couple of screws on each side of her temple. She swivelled aside the top of her head. Alice leaned forward to peer into the gaping skull and found inside a loosely packed mound of soil through which a million termites were scuttling, and no doubt passing questions and answers and answers and questions to each other.

"So you're using the beanery system?" asked Alice.

"I wouldn't know anything about beans," answered Celia. "I think I must be an automaton. You know what an automaton is, don't you, Alice?"

"Is it a toy that can move without being pushed or dragged?"

"That is correct, and that is what I have become. I am the automated version of you, Alice. The word automation comes from the ancient Greek; it means that I'm *self-moving;* it means that I'm self-improving. In point of fact, I've improved myself so much . . . I've become rather more intelligent than a human being."

"But surely," Alice said, "in order to equal the thinking of a single human mind, a termite mound would have to be as large as the world itself." (Alice was only borrowing this knowledge from Captain Ramshackle, not really stealing it, so we can forgive her for this slight copycattering, surely?)

"Indeed it would be," replied Celia (referring to the mound-size), "but that argument fails to remember the ingenuity of Pablo the sculptor. Pablo has managed to breed the termites down to the size of pencils."

"But pencils are so much *longer* than termites," Alice argued.

"Not if they're used up from the tip and nibbled down from the eraser. Eventually a pencil will meet itself in the middle and then it will vanish. Just like us, Alice! Perhaps we faded away from both ends until we met in our middles and then we vanished! I'm a work of art, did you know that?" Celia twirled around quite proudly as she said this. "I'm terbo-charged!"

"Celia, why are you dropping the letter T from the word?" Alice asked.

"Because that's how the future people say it," Celia replied. "You do know that we're in the future now, Alice? I must have slipped from your fingers whilst falling through the tunnel of clock-numbers. I therefore entered the future at an earlier date than you did. I landed in 1998 a whole week before you. I had grown to my present size, but I was still only a doll. I could not move at all, or even think for myself. Pablo the sculptor claims that he found me lying in this very garden, in a briar of roses."

"Did Mister Pablo plant this knot garden?" Alice asked.

"He most certainly did. Pablo's hobby is to make terbots, you see? The Civil Serpents look down upon this hobby; they think it very unreal. Only by promising that his creations would be trapped forever in a garden of knots and guarded by snakes could Pablo convince the serpents that his work be allowed. It was Pablo that put the computermites in my skull. Alice, my dear, it was as if I had woken up from a long, long sleep of doll-ness. I came alive!"

"Celia, I'm very glad that you're alive," stated Alice, "but I simply must get you and Whippoorwill and myself back to Great Aunt Ermintrude's house in time for my two o'clock writing lesson." Just then an almighty commotion took place beyond the knot garden; red and white lights flashed in the sky above the hedgerows and a piercing cry howled through the morning, followed by what sounded very much like a police-man's whistle being blown. "Whatever's happening now?" cried Alice.

"Maybe it's something to do with the Jigsaw Murder," replied Celia.

"You know about the Jigsaw Murder?" a surprised Alice enquired.

"I don't know much about the case," Celia replied, "but I *do* know that Whippoorwill isn't too happy with the sudden disturbance." Indeed, the parrot was flapping his green-and-yellow wings in a chaotic pattern that Captain Ramshackle would have been very proud of. It was these movements that caused Alice to remember certain words that the badgerman had spoken. "Celia," she asked, "would you happen to know the whereabouts of a certain Professor Gladys Chrowdingler by any chance?"

"I'm afraid I don't. What does she study?"

"The Mysteries of Time."

"That does sound useful. We must do our very best to find this Professor."

"What about an ellipsis? Do you know what one of those is?"

"An ellipsis? Isn't that the sister of an ellipse?"

"Celia, I think your computermites must be on holiday. Oh, if only I'd asked Captain Ramshackle where Professor Chrowdingler lived! But I was in such a hurry to find Whippoorwill. At least I've managed one good job this day!" With these words Alice reached out to lift Whippoorwill off Celia's shoulder. But the parrot was too quick for her: with a flickering fluttering of feathers he managed to fly off Celia's shoulder just before Alice's fingers reached him. He flew above the hedgerows over towards where the lights were flashing.

"Oh goodness!" exclaimed Alice. "Whippoorwill has once again escaped! However shall we find him this time? This garden is so tightly knotted."

"I think I may know a way," Celia answered, taking hold of Alice's hand. "Follow me."

ADVENTURES

IN A

GARDEN SHED

THE Automated Alice led the Real-life Alice over to where a small garden shed was sitting in one curvy corner of the maze's centre circle. (I say "sitting" because the garden shed really did appear to be *sitting* on the grass, and rather awkwardly at that!) Above the closed door, a painted sign read: OGDEN'S REVERSE BUTCHERY. The garden shed was tilted precariously to one side, with many planks missing, and even more of them just about to fall off. From within came a terrible racket: a terrible banging! and a clattering! and then a terrible walloping! and then a terrible cursing cry! and then yet more banging! and clattering! and, indeed, walloping! To Alice's eyes, it looked very much like the garden shed had been dropped from a great height: indeed, she was certain that the shed hadn't even been there when she had first entered the centre of the maze, but how could a common-or-garden garden shed simply appear out of nowhere?

Celia was pounding on the shed's door: "Pablo, Pablo!" the doll croaked. "Let me in, please. Stop making that terrible racket!"

And the racket *was* stopped for a second, as a gruff and angry voice answered from the interior, "But I like making a terrible racket! It's my job! It's my *Art!*" The shed's door was then flung open with such violence that it almost flew off its hinges, and standing in the doorway was an extremely overgrown man. He was the first completely *normal* man that Alice had seen that morning, even if he was very, very large, and dressed in a blood-smeared butcher's apron. He was holding a terrible racket in his hands.

(I must add at this point that the terrible racket he was holding was a tennis racket, and it was *terrible* because the man had obviously been making it that very morning out of bits and various pieces: bits of old sideboards and pencil-cases and various pieces of string and wire and shoelaces. It really did look most unsuitable for the civilised game of tennis.)

"Celia! My little terbot!" the big man cried. "What in the blazing mazes are you doing off your snake-guarded podium?"

"Pablo, may I introduce Alice," Celia calmly responded. "She has rescued me from the snake's hold."

"But that's impossible!" said Pablo.

"Good morning, Mister Odgen," said Alice, on her best behaviour.

"A girl! At last!" sobbed Pablo Ogden. "Another human being! It's been so long . . . so very, very long . . . you'd better come in. Quickly, quickly! . . . before the snakes come crawling!"

Once Alice and her automated sister were inside the garden shed, Pablo pulled the door shut with a vicious bang that caused the whole structure to shake. Alice really did think that the shed was going to collapse around them into splinters and dust, but somehow it kept itself together. It was very cramped inside, especially with the hulking Pablo bent in half over his cumbersome workbench, and with all the tools that were stored there, and because of the large ship's wheel and compass that were fixed to the floor. And then there was Pablo's latest terbot creation, which quite by itself took up more than two thirds of the room. "Magnificent! Isn't he?" Pablo asked upon seeing Alice's wild-eyed stare. "My greatest work. His name is James Marshall Hentrails, Jimi for short. Well then, young girl . . . what do you think of him?"

The lumbering sculpture looked like a pile of rubbish assembled into the vaguest resemblance of a man. His legs were made from spindly gutter-pipes; his body from a wash-board and a mangle (all covered up with a well-read jacket woven out of discarded book covers); his arms were borrowed from the legs of a long-gone-to-salt-and-pepper chicken, all jointed up with brass wire and ending in a fine pair of puppet's hands; his head was (disquietingly) almost human, a doll's face of blackened skin on the top of which languished a long and shaggy knotted haircut made out of the ripped-up legs of a pair of ebony corduroy trousers. In other words: a perfect pile of rubbish.

"Why is his name Mister Hentrails?" Alice asked, delaying her opinion.

"You know what entrails are, don't you, Alice?" Pablo responded, whilst unfastening a small door in the sculpture's stomach.

"Of course I do," Alice replied, quite embarrassed. "Entrails are the . . . they are the . . . well, entrails are the insides of a . . . the insides of a . . . a . . . ."

Alice could not make herself say the words, and very relieved she was to let Pablo answer his own question: "Exactly, Alice!

Entrails are the insides of a cow! And therefore . . ." and here Pablo swung open the sculpture's stomach with a flourish, "hentrails are the insides of a chicken!"

"Urghhh!" Alice squealed, "how horrid!" For within the sculpture's stomach lay a knotted mass of blood and flesh.

"This is how a terbot feeds," Pablo elucidated. "Now come on, girl, what *do* you think of my latest masterpiece? Your honest opinion, now."

"A child of six-and-five-quarters could have made this sculpture!"

"Oh thank you, little Alice!" Pablo cried. "A child could have made this! Why, that's exactly the effect I was hoping for. Only at the age of six-and-five-quarters are we truly at home with our fantasies! The artist, you see, must travel backwards in time. To become, once again, a child of dreams."

"But Mister Odgen," said Alice, "that's exactly what I want to do. To travel backwards in time. Please find a way out of this garden for Celia and me."

"A way out for Celia, you ask?" Pablo muttered. "But that's amazingly impossible! A terbot leaving the knot garden? Why, the snakes would strangle you both! It's the written rulings. No, no and no! Terbots are bound to the garden. Even my latest and greatest creation, James Marshall Hentrails himself, why even he is doomed to stillness once the snakes get hold of him. There's no way out of the garden for a terbot. That's the unliving truth."

"Pablo, why are you making such a terrible tennis racket?" asked Celia.

"It might look like a terrible racket," replied Pablo, "but really it's a guitar. Although, it does make a *terrible* racket."

"How so?" Celia enquired.

"Watch closely," Pablo answered, slotting the tennis racket into the outstretched hands of James Marshall Hentrails, and then flipping open the top of the sculpture's skull. "Now, all that Jimi needs is a little brain power." Pablo opened up a drawer in his workbench, and reached in with a garden trowel, to dig out a large scoopful of thick, black soil. "Aha! My lovely beauties!" Pablo announced, shovelling the soil into the hollow of the terbot's head.

"Are there computermites in that soil?" Alice asked.

"Pablillions of them! The tiniest computermites in the whole world! My own invention. Watch closely . . ." Pablo closed up the skull with a loud and violent squelch, and then turned a switch on the terbot's neck.

Nothing happened.

James Marshall Hentrails made not a move.

"It takes the mites a while to warm up," Pablo apologised, with a sigh. "Maybe there's a wurm in his workings. Oh dear."

"Pablo, we really do need to get out of the garden," Celia said during another awkward pause; "Alice is so very desperate to get back home." Pablo was nudging at the elbows of James Marshall Hentrails, paying no attention to Celia's urgings.

"Alice and I have come from the past, and, if we don't get home soon, it may be too late . . ."

"Too late?" Pablo murmured, "too late for the past?" He

turned away from his beloved sculpture for a second. "How can one be too late for the past?"

"Alice is a *girl*," Celia responded. "When was the last time you saw a girl?"

Pablo looked long and deep into Alice's eyes and then answered, "Years and years ago. Years and years! Not since the years before the Newmonia."

"But why should pneumonia cause such a lack of girls?" asked Alice.

"*New*monia!" Pablo screamed at Alice. "Not *pneu*monia! You silly creature! There's no P in Newmonia."

"But the P is silent in pneumonia," Alice explained (holding her patience).

"Why can't you listen properly, Alice? The Newmonia is a terrible disease that allows animals and humans to get mixed into *new* combinations."

"Like Captain Ramshackle?" suggested Alice.

"Exactly like the badgerman. You're one of the last of your kind, girl! So pure, so very pure. Keep a tight hold of that. If you *are* a real girl, that is?"

"How dare you?" Alice protested. "I'm *real*, I tell you. Why, I might well ask if you are a *real* butcher, as your sign outside proclaims? Because I suspect that you're not really a butcher at all."

"I used to be a real butcher," Pablo responded, "in my youth, but I became tired of simply cutting up creatures, so I became a reverse butcher instead."

"And what is one of those?" Alice asked.

"Can't you work it out, girl?" Pablo asked, whilst beginning to close up the stomach-door of James Marshall Hentrails. "A reverse butcher is an artisan of the flesh who reconstructs creatures out of their butchered parts."

"Wait a minute, Mister Odgen!" cried Alice (having noticed a certain tiny something within the sculpture's giblets), "please don't shut up Jimi's stomach just yet! I do believe that *this* is mine!" She reached into the soft, damp, warm interior of the giblets (shivering from the squelchiness!) to pluck free a small piece of jagged wood that rested just to the North of the liver and the kidneys. "This is a piece of my jigsaw zoo," Alice said, bringing the bit of wood into the light. It very much corresponded to the eyes and the beak of a chicken (although why the London Zoo should want to display a common domestic fowl was quite beyond Alice's understanding). She added the fourth and feathery item to the other three jigsaw pieces in her pinafore pocket.

"Maybe that's why Jimi Hentrails was so slow to come to life," Pablo pontificated. "He had a splinter in his stomach. That would surely slow him down." And indeed, at that very moment the sculpture did make a small attempt at life: his spindly limbs jerked into a spasm of stunted dance. "Alice, my dear girl!" Pablo cried. "You have cured my creation! How can I possibly thank you?"

"Take me home," Alice replied immediately, "take me back to the past."

"To the past we are heading!" announced Pablo Ogden, working at some complicated levers that sprouted from the shed's floor. With the manipulation of these levers, a frightening number of iron cables started to move along a series of pulleys that were fixed to the shed's ceiling: from the pulleys the cables fed into an array of holes cut into the shed's floor. "Hold on tight, my friends!" Pablo shouted above the resulting clanking din.

And then the garden shed started to move!

The garden shed started to quiver quite haphazardly and Alice was flung to the floor as the wooden world of her present life lifted up into the air. Celia and James Marshall Hentrails were both thrown to one side as the shed *elevated itself above the garden!* "Whatever's happening?" screamed Alice, clinging desperately to the workbench.

"The garden shed is taking a little stroll, of course," replied Pablo Ogden, as he struggled with the ship's wheel, in order to swing the shed around. "The shed has grown her legs!" There was a trapdoor in the shed's floor, with some small holes in it, through which a few drifts of smoke were rising. "That's the steam given off by the shed's legs," stated Pablo, "take a little peek, Alice." Pablo swung open the trapdoor and Alice peered through the gaping hole, only to see that far below her the garden was passing by at an ever-quickening pace!

"Oh my goodness!" cried Alice. (And well she might, for just at that very moment the garden shed *lurched achingly* to one side and Alice felt herself slipping through the trapdoor.) "Oh my double goodness!" Alice cried once again. (As well she doubly might, because now she was falling out of the shed!)

(And the garden was a long, long way down and down . . .)

Luckily, just as her body started this gardenwards journey

into breath-gulping air, Alice felt a strong hand gripping itself
around her ankle. She was now suspended *upside-down!* from
the lip of the shed's trapdoor and from this advantageous position she could see in full detail the legs of the garden shed: they
were the legs of a chicken, albeit mechanised and grown to a
monstrous size; the legs were steaming and stepping over the
hedgerows. The garden shed really was walking! "So this is how
Mister Ogden manages to get around the knot garden," Alice
said to herself. "He doesn't get *around* it, he gets *above* it." Alice
also saw various tools falling upwards past her from the trapdoor, including a hammer and a hacksaw. "And this is why I
came across so many tools in the knot garden," she added to
her upside-down self, "and this is how I found the hacksaw that
enabled me to find Celia Doll." Alice also saw, in the upside-
down far distance, Whippoorwill the very naughty parrot flying
over towards an iron gate that marked the exit from the maze.

"Whippoorwill!" she called out, "you come back here, this
minute!"

The parrot of course paid Alice no mind. How could he?
The parrot was a thousand wing-beats away and Alice was by
then being dragged back into the uncertain safety of the lumbering garden shed. It was Celia who had clutched at her ankle
at the last second of falling. "Follow that parrot!" cried Alice,
pointing through the doorway.

And follow that distant parrot Pablo did, working the shed's
controls so that the walking, wobbling construction on a chick-
en's overgrown legs made a run for the iron-gated exit. James
Marshall Hentrails was meanwhile strumming his puppet's fin-

gers across the strings of his guitar, making a horrible blast of
notes arise from the instrument (SPERANNGGGUH! FIZZLE!
WHEEEE! SNAZZBLAT! QWEET!). Alice covered her ears.
"Oh my!" she said, "what a terrible racket!"

"I told you so, didn't I?" Pablo bellowed, over the noise. "He
calls this tune 'Little Miss Bonkers.' "

"Excuse me," screamed Alice, from behind her hands, "what
is that word?"

"Which word?"

"That Bonkers word."

"Bonkers? You've never heard of bonkers?"

"No, never."

"Oh, it's used all the time in Manchester. It means Bananas."

"Bananas!"

"Yes. As in, Completely Bananas."

"Oh, I see," shouted Alice, not seeing at all, because Jimi
Hentrails had now started to sing, drawling his lyrics between
each outburst of guitar-strangling:

> *Little Miss Bonkers!* (BLISSSTUMB! TANG! SHEMUFFLE!)
>> *Lost*
> *In a* (MANGLE!) *of time and a knotted bind.*
>> (TWANGLE!) *Freed a friend and awoke to find*
>>> *The love that conquers.* (JUZZ! JUZZ! KERJANGLE!)
> (FUNKY WOOFGOSH!)
>>> *Sidestepping the snakes to be tossed*
>> *As Pablo concurs*
>>> *Completely* (KLONK!) *bonkers!*

Jimi Hentrails then went into a long and loud guitar solo that made the garden shed shudder even more. Alice clung on tightly to the quivering workbench, as she shouted to Pablo, "What kind of art is it that you craft, Mister Ogden? Because your latest creation is not making any kind of sense!"

"I call my art *Skewedism*," Pablo stated, working his controls, "which allows me to make creatures out of rudity. Indeed, I used to call my art *Rudism,* and then *Crudism,* but those labels seemed too crudely, rudely obvious. Before that I was making *Gluedism,* where all the parts are glued together, and some time before that, *Cluedism,* where I had only the faintest clue as to what I was doing. But then I realised that I didn't have a clue at all, and I started to brood upon my doings; so then I called my art *Broodism.* But that didn't seem to fit at all. So I called it *Shoedism,* because all my sculptures seemed to be wearing shoes. And then *Shrewdism,* because wasn't I being very shrewd in the making of them? And then *Cubism,* because I was assembling the cubes of moments lost. But that label seemed to me so limiting, because by then I was making creatures out of creatures! So I called my art *Zoodism.* And then *Fludism,* because I couldn't stop sneezing. And then *Chewedism,* because I couldn't stop chewing. And then *Bluedism,* because I couldn't stop painting everything blue. *Ewedism:* sculptures of female sheep. *Foodism:* sculptures of dinnertime. I've also been through *Moodism, Brewedism,* all the young *Dudeisms, Judeism, Lewdism, Nudism* and *Pseudism.* I then made a stab at *Whodism,* because who in the mazes was I anyway, to be making such illegal creatures? And then finally, after many a strange *Queuedism,* whilst waiting for a proper label, I finally settled upon *Skewedism,* because my mind is skew-whiff with so much diverseness. This is why the Civil Serpents hate my work so: they can't stand anything that is even a little bit skewed."

James Marshall Hentrails finished his crazy solo and began the second verse of his song, accessoried by creeping guitar:

> *Little Miss Anagram!* (ZING! ZANG! QWERTYUIOP!)
> > *Completely bananas!*
> > (ASDFGH! JKL!) *Polygon pyjama jam!*
> (ZX! CVB! NM!)
> > *Awake from your dramas* (!@£$%^&*!)
> > *Forever mañanas!*

The word *polygon* only reminded Alice of how far away her parrot was. "The garden gate is looming close, Alice," shouted Pablo, over the singing.

Indeed, the shed had now folded up its chickeny legs, in order to squat itself down, some twenty yards from the knot garden's exit. Alice had one last question, as she ran towards the door, and it was this: "Pablo, what was that last word that Jimi sang?"

"What word?" answered Pablo.

"That mañanas word."

"It's Spanish for tomorrow, Alice. The singer is asking us to celebrate the Forever Tomorrows. Wouldn't you like that?"

"I wouldn't like that, at all!" said Alice, as Celia and herself stepped out, onto the grass, "because yesterday is where I want to be."

(JOING! SHULEEOINNNGH! BLOZZ BLOZZ BLOZZ!)

Jimi Hentrails was still playing up a storm, as Pablo called after the two girls, "Watch out for the snakes, Alice: they won't like Celia leaving the garden . . ."

Imagine, after taking only a few steps over the dewy grass, Alice heard a terrible *swishing* sound from behind her; and then imagine her surprise when seemingly a *hundred slithering snakes* came rushing out of the hedgerows, all of them extremely keen to take a fangly bite at her ankles!

THE LONG

PAW OF THE LAW

SNAKES, snakes, snakes!

Everywhere all around Alice a swissshing and a hisssing noise could be heard as a hundred-knot of sssnakes ssslithered and sssibilanted themselves through the undergrowth. It was now thirty minutes past seven o'clock in the morning and the Real-life Alice was being viciously dragged towards the knot garden's exit gate by Celia, the Automated Alice. The sun was rising over and above the hedgerows, illuminating the rainbowed scales of the collected ranks of the Under Assistant Civil Serpents. Alice glanced behind at a sudden scrunching noise to see the walking shed of Pablo Ogden lumbering off, back towards the centre of the garden. And then she was running towards the iron gates and jumping over many a snake in her journey. "All I seem to be doing in 1998," Alice said to herself whilst running (and jumping) alongside Celia, "is *running!* Running, running, running! It was never like this in 1860: why, in the afternoon of that year, I could not even be bothered to get out of my armchair. Not even for a writing lesson! Maybe everything is so much *faster* in the future? At this rate I shall never catch my breath, let alone my parrot!"

"Quickly, Alice, quickly!" Celia cried, fearful of the snakes dragging her back into the garden. "The gates are just ahead of us."

They made it only just in time. Celia wrenched open the iron gates with her terbo-charged arms (even as the myriad snakes were biting at her porcelain ankles) and then pushed Alice through into the next episode. Celia clanged the gates shut behind her (squashing one of the snakes' heads in the closing process). "Jolly bad luck, Mister Snakified Under Assistant!" Celia sang, quite gleefully.

And that was how Alice and Celia made their entrance into the streets of Manchester.

OOO

Alice had never seen such a hellish noise before, such a tumul-titude, such a cacophonous display of *wailings and screechings!* And so very early in the morning! Why this was even worse than the terrible racket that James Marshall Hentrails had made upon his terrible racket. Alice and Celia were now stand-ing at the side of an extremely busy thoroughfare; behind them the gates to the knot garden were being hissed at madly by the frustrated snakes. In front of them were hundreds of moaning metal horses, who breathed out a fulsome wind of smelly gases from their hind ends as they sped along the road (at more than twenty miles per hour!). Clinging tightly to the saddle of each metal horse was a person (not one of which looked entirely human).

"My goodness!" cried Alice to Celia. "What a *pong!* I've never seen so many horses before."

"These are not horses," said Celia, "these are carriages."

"Well they certainly look a little like horses."

"These vehicles are horseless carriages."

"How do you know that the carriages are horseless?" asked Alice.

"Because they haven't got any real horses drawing them."

"I didn't know that real horses could draw. Can they also paint?"

"Alice! You must know what I mean!" Celia cried. "A *horseless* carriage is what the people of the future call a carriage that isn't being pulled by a horse."

"Is that similar to a pianoless lampshade?" asked Alice.

"Whatever's a pianoless lampshade?" asked Celia.

"Why, it's a lampshade that isn't being played by a piano, of course."

"Alice! I'm getting rather tired of your loopiness!" Celia replied. "Only by working together can we escape from this future world and thereby make our way back to the past. We are the not-quite twins, the sisters of the corkscrew. Your feelings, my logic—Girl and Doll; only by this shared route may we travel back home. Don't you see that yet?"

Alice didn't see it, mainly because she was too busy studying the lights and cries rising above the houses on the opposite side of the road. Alice just knew that Whippoorwill would be attracted to those colours and noises, and (having spotted a small gap in the rushing traffic) Alice stepped out into the road. Oh dear: one of the ever-so-horseless carriages nearly knocked her down. In fact, that passing vehicle clipped Alice on the elbow! "*Yeeooohhh!*" Alice yeeooohhhed, falling back onto the pavement, "that hurt!"

"The proper name for a horseless carriage is an automated horse," Celia coldly responded, whilst rubbing at Alice's arm with her porcelain fingers. "But in these yet-to-come days, the people are far too busy to use the full name for things; so they call their transportations *auto-horses*. Which they sometimes even further shorten to simply *autos.*"

"Well, that may be so," Alice replied (wincingly, on account of her pain), "but in our day, we called a horse a horse and a carriage a carriage, and there was no such thing as a horseless carriage, because a carriage could not move unless it had a horse in front of it!"

"Alice, won't you please admit that we're trapped in the future now. We must learn the latest lessons. Believe me, my dear, we are currently facing a drive of auto-horses."

"I hate lessons," sulked Alice as she nursed her injured elbow, "but at least I know that the collective noun for horses is a herd." (How proud Alice was, to have pointed this out to Celia.)

"I think you'll find, my somewhat pale human companion," Celia gently suggested, "that you can have a herd of cattle, a herd of bison, or even a herd of elephants. But you cannot have a herd of horses. You may, however, have a drove of horses. But when the horses are automated, they become a drive. And we are still facing a galloping drive of autos."

"Oh, Celia! You think you know every single thing."

"Well, one doesn't like to boast; but you must concede that the name auto-horses perfectly suits these carriages. Why, one need only examine their legs . . ." Alice did examine their legs (having completely missed Celia's correct usage of the ellipsis) and she had to admit to herself (because she didn't want Celia to think she was right *all* the time) that they certainly looked more than a little like an automated horse's legs. "To my terbotmind," Celia added, proudly, "the people of the future have wedded the horse to the carriage: these are horsey carriages."

"Oh but look, Celia!" Alice interrupted, shrugging off Celia's healing hands. "The autos have snakes wriggling above their eyes!"

"Don't you worry, Alice," replied Celia, "those snakes are there in case it rains; they're called windscreen vipers."

There was no possible way to cross the road. The autohorses were riding along, nose to tail, tail to nose: a constant creaking and neighing of metal and noise. "If they're not careful," Celia announced finally, "these riders are going to cause a horse-crash. We need to find a Zebra Crossing."

"Whatever's a Zebra Crossing?" Alice asked.

"A place in the road where even a zebra can cross. It's one of the Civil Serpents' better rulings—"

"There's one!" cried Alice. And indeed there was: there *was* a zebra, crossing the road a long, long way away from Alice and Celia. "Follow that zebra!" Alice called out. "He's a piebald, actually!" Celia added. Alice didn't bother to ask what a bald pie was doing in the conversation, she was far too busy running along towards where the zebra was crossing the road. "Look at that, Celia!" she called out as the pair of them reached the spot, "Whippoorwill is perched on the zebra's shoulder!"

The parrot *was* perched on the zebra's shoulder. And, by that stripy transport, he was working his way towards the other side of the road. (Alice never thought to ask herself why the parrot simply didn't *fly* across the road, she was far too used to his wayward nature by now.) And indeed, just then Whippoorwill fluttered his green-and-yellow wings in quite a shameless display and twisted his head around through one-hundred-and-eighty degrees in order to squak at Alice, "Why did the Catgirl cross the road?"

Alice felt sure that the parrot was laughing at her, so she didn't even attempt an answer to this latest riddle. The zebra was looking rather scared during his passage between the parted ranks of the auto-horses (and wouldn't you, if you were a horse's relative in a horseless society?). It wasn't a real zebra of course: Alice had learnt enough about this future Manchester to know that nothing was really real anymore. Oh no, following the effects of the Newmonia (if Pablo Ogden was to be believed) Whippoorwill was riding upon the shoulder of a zebraman: a black-and-white-striped combination of the human and the zebra. This zebra-man had by now almost succeeded in crossing, so Alice nervously stepped into the road after him. The riders of the auto-horses shouted all manner of curses at Alice, the worst of which came from a sweating fat pigboy: "What in the mud-bath is that?!" he snorted, "some kind of a girl crossing the road!"

"Where are we?" Alice asked of Celia, whilst only a little less than half-way across (and doing her very best to ignore the insults).

"We are currently crossing a thoroughfare called Wilmslow Road," Celia replied, "in a place called Rusholme, a small village some few miles away from the centre of Manchester." Ahead of them now could be seen a large building with the words PALACE OF CHIMERA written large and golden across its frontage, and underneath these, FLUTTERING TODAY: FLIPPETY FLOPPETY COMES UNSTUCK!

"Why do they call this village Rush Home?" asked Alice, a little further along in the crossing. "It seems to me that the people of Manchester are rushing away from their homes."

"Exactly so, Alice. And in eight hours' time they will commence to rush home, after finishing their day's work. They call these twin times the rush hours."

The zebraman had by now managed to completely cross the road. The auto-horses started up a snarling and braying, as though they wanted to *eat* Alice and Celia alive, and then sprang forwards in a rapid burst of metallic clankings! Celia Doll firmly grabbed hold of Alice's hand and *started to walk faster than anybody had ever walked before!* Alice felt she was flying, so quickly did Celia move. "Celia!" Alice cried, "where in the future did you learn to walk so quickly?" But her words were lost to the frightening wind that Celia created in her rush to get away from the accelerating auto-horses. "Oh well," said

Alice to herself, "I suppose if I were an Automated Alice, I also would be able to run as quickly." Just then the screaming drive of horsey carriages fairly pounced upon the pair of them, aiming to squash!

Alice and Celia did manage to cross the road of course, if only by the hairs on their smallest toenails. (And a good job too, otherwise this fable would be a very sorry story indeed. Why, I'm not even half-way through Alice's adventures in the future yet. No, no; it would not do to have my principal actors quite so easily squashed by metal hooves!)

Upon gaining the safety of the opposite pavement, Alice lunged forward to grab at Whippoorwill, but all she managed to grab hold of was a single green-and-yellow tail feather, which she plucked clean from the bird! Whippoorwill himself, despite lacking a tail feather, flew off quite easily from the zebraman's shoulder, disappearing over the roof of the Palace of Chimera and into a hive of houses. The zebraman trotted off in the same direction, leaving Alice to clutch desperately at the parrot's lonely feather. "Do you think, Celia," Alice then asked, "that Great Aunt Ermintrude will be satisfied with a single feather from her lost parrot?"

"I think not, Alice," Celia replied. "But look at this!" Celia had bent down to pick up a little piece of something from the ground. "The zebraman must have dropped this in his hurry to get away." It was a wooden piece from a jigsaw, portraying a rippling pattern of black-and-white stripes. Celia handed it to Alice.

"This is yet another missing piece from my jigsaw of London Zoo," Alice proclaimed. "This belongs in the zebra house." Alice took the piece and placed it in the pocket of her pinafore, with the other four she had already gathered. "Are we anywhere near Didsbury, Celia?" she then asked.

"We are," the doll replied, "but we are going in the opposite direction. Why do you ask?"

"Because that is where my Great Aunt lives, or should I say *once* lived, and we have to find our way back there."

"But not just now, dear Alice."

"For once, dear Celia, I entirely agree with you."

The pair of them set off in pursuit of Whippoorwill, entering the hive of houses. They very quickly found themselves lost again, of course. The trouble was this: every house was identical, and every street was identical. And every street was tightly knotted around every other street. The whole world it seemed was identically identical and twisted around itself. It was yet another knotty problem for Alice to unravel. But the lights were flashing into the glistening morning sky and the siren-calls and the whistlings came trumpeting from the hidden streets. In the end, it was only by relying on Celia's superior judgement that Alice managed to find the place where the noises and the lights were coming from.

Imagine this scene, if you will, dear reader . . .

A drive of police-autos (horseless carriages belonging to the police) were parked inside the centre of these all-too-identical houses. A crowd of animal-people was clogging up the street: goatboys and sheepgirls, elephantmen and batwomen. Alice

nudged her way through the strange zoo of spectators. "Can you please tell me what is happening here?" she asked of the nearest policeman.

"A second Jigsaw Murder has taken place," the policeman gravely replied, his furry body full of trembles. "A catgirl this time."

It was only when Alice noticed the policeman's fur trembling that she realised that this policeman was really a policedog; or rather a policedogman. Yet another victim of the Newmonia, of course. Alice tried to push her way past the policedogman to where a lumpy something on the ground was lying quite still and morbid, under a white bedsheet. Only a single gingery furred cat's paw and claw protruded free, to rest, lifelessly, on the pavement.

"How sad," whispered Alice, in horror. (For Alice had a pet kitten of her own, far away in the distant past. Sweet, sweet Dinah of forgotten years!)

Just then another policedogman came loping towards Alice. This dogman was growling at the other dogmen, telling them all to get a move on, and at the double-quick! He was obviously in charge. Alice could tell this, not only from his barked-out orders, but also from the fact that he  wore a suit, a *tailored* suit at that, whilst all the other policedogmen wore blue police uniforms over their canine bodies. "And who are you?" this boss-of-all-dogs asked of Alice. He had a face of finely furred colours: a broad and brown stripe running all the way along a creamy, whiskered snout.

"I'm Alice," replied Alice.

"And I am Inspector Jack Russell of the Greater Manchester Police. What are you doing here, Alice?"

"Well, Inspector Russell . . . I do believe that's my parrot on your shoulder."

Inspector Jack Russell did indeed have Whippoorwill perched on his shoulder. "This parrot is guilty of hindering the police in their inquiries," Jack Russell barked, "and I want him *off my shoulder right this minute!*"

"Whippoorwill, come fly to me," Alice sang, only to see the parrot unlodge himself from Jack Russell's shoulder and then fly away, not towards her but to the ever-brightening morning sky that flittered above the houses: the parrot was heading for the centre of Manchester.

"Pardon me, my stripy horseman!" Jack Russell growled at the zebraman who had suddenly appeared on the scene, nudging his wet nose at the dead catgirl's bedsheet. "Don't you realise that you're hindering my investigation of a caticide?"

"Whatever's a catty side?" asked Alice.

"The murder of a catgirl, of course," answered the Inspector. (Which gave Alice the answer to Whippoorwill's last riddle: why did the catgirl cross the road? To get to the catty side, of course!)

To get to her death.

"The victim's name," Jack Russell continued, "was Whiskers Macduff. This is the second of the Jigsaw Murders. The first victim was a young spiderboy, name of Quentin Tarantula. He was a Chimera artiste, famous for his violent, celebratory portrayal of the criminal life. I must admit that I won't be shedding any tears at his demise. That kind of Chimera show shouldn't be allowed."

"What is a Chimera show, exactly?" Alice asked.

"What's Chimera?!" howled Jack Russell. "Where have *you* been for the last five years?"

"I haven't been anywhere for the last five years," Alice replied. "In fact, I haven't been anywhere for the last one hundred and thirty-eight years!"

Inspector Jack Russell ignored this remark. "Chimera is where they play the flutters, of course."

"The flutters!" smiled Alice. "That sounds like fun!"

"Fun!" yowled the Inspector. "Oh no: Chimera is a blatant pandering to the sickly needs of the common herd, a fluttering of evil pictures on a wall!"

"Is Chimera a little like a lantern show?" asked Alice.

"And the newspapers dare to ask why the crime numbers are soaring!" barked Jack Russell.

"What has this to do with the Jigsaw Murders?" requested Alice.

"Quentin Tarantula was a maker of Chimera. Surely I explained that already? He was murdered, and then all of his eight legs were sliced off and stitched to his head! Stitched, I say! And this pathetic catgirl has suffered the same fate: her body parts have been rearranged."

Alice felt quite sick.

"This is why we call these killings the Jigsaw Murders. Take a look at this . . ." Inspector Jack Russell opened his paws to dangle a small piece of wood in front of Alice's face. "We found this clutched in the spiderboy's legs." It was another jigsaw piece! Alice recognised the fragment: the missing picture of a deadly spider from her long-ago puzzle of London Zoo.

"That's *my* jigsaw piece!" Alice cried.

"Is it indeed?" Jack Russell replied. "Well then, take a look at this . . ." And with this ellipsis the policedogman prised open the only exposed claw of the currently dead catgirl, revealing yet a further jigsaw piece hidden there. "Does *this* jigsaw piece also belong to you, I wonder?" he asked, brandishing a crooked portion of the golden eye of a cat.

"That *is* also mine!" Alice said.

"Alice the human-girl," Inspector Jack Russell coldly growled, "I am hereby arresting you for probable involvement in the Jigsaw Murders. I believe you to be in league with the Ramshackle badgerman, our main suspect, and that together you have brought about these rearranging killings. The Civil Serpents will be most keen to interrogate you."

Just then it started to rain!

To rain and rain and rain.

An astonished (and drenched) Alice felt a pair of police manacles folding around her wrists, and at the very same time she saw Captain Ramshackle himself being led on leads by a cluster of policedogmen. The badgerman looked at Alice as he passed by. "Alice, you *know* that I'm innocent," he muttered in the downpour. "Won't you please help me?"

"Good Captain, I will do my utmost to help you," Alice replied, whilst being dogmanhandled herself onto the back of a police-auto. "I shall prove us both innocent yet . . ."

The last thing that Alice saw as the auto-horse galloped off with her was the porcelain look on Celia Doll's face from the crowd of dripping spectators. "Oh Celia!" Alice cried out, "I'm losing you all over again. Whatever shall become of us now?"

Alice's ride on the auto-horse's back was a terrifying rain-beaten gallop into the centre of Manchester. Wilmslow Road changed into Oxford Road, towards the centre, and many a wonder Alice passed on her journey into Manchester, surrounded as she was by a skidding and flashing drive of other auto-horses, all carrying their very own intrepid riders (or should that be drivers?). Alice passed the Infirmary and the University: she also passed the Central Library and the great Town Hall of Manchester.

The police auto-horse eventually drew to a standstill at the Police Station, opposite the Town Hall.

LANGUISHING

IN JAIL

FIVE

minutes later Alice found herself being locked up inside a minuscule jail cell in the cellar below the Police Station. "This is not fair!" she shouted to Inspector Jack Russell as he forced her into the cell. "I'm innocent! Let me free!"

"The Over Assistant Civil Serpent will be along shortly," Jack Russell briefly replied. "You may plead your case to her."

Inspector Jack Russell left the cell and clanged the door shut behind him.

Alice could hear the key turning in the lock, just so that she now knew she was completely alone.

A long, long time passed and nobody at all came to visit her, not even a Civil Serpent. Hours and hours must have passed. Alice was feeling very lonely and unwanted—very much unloved. The jail cell contained no furniture other than a rude bed and no windows other than a tiny, barred hole set high up on the wall, through which Alice could catch only a glint of distant rainlight. Alice was so very hungry, not having eaten since lunchtime. That's lunchtime, 1860, by the way. Alice was left to her own devices. Of course, Alice's devices amounted to nothing more than Whippoorwill's plucked-out tail feather, and five small pieces from a jigsaw of London Zoo, which offered hardly any comfort at all (especially to the stomach).

Alice quickly became bored of doing nothing at all, so she decided to play with her feather and her jigsaw pieces. First of all she placed the feather on the bed's rough blanket. Then she dug deep into her pinafore pocket to find the five jigsaw pieces she had collected in her travels so far: the termite, the badger, the snake, the chicken and the zebra. She laid these pieces face-up in a circle surrounding the green-and-yellow feather.

"Now then," Alice said to herself, "what game shall I play with you? Shall I play Feather-Escape-the-Zoo? Or shall I play Zoo-Catch-a-Feather?"

Alice moved the jigsaw pieces around the feather, and then the feather amongst the jigsaw pieces, and then she threw the whole lot of them to the floor!

"Oh! What difference does it make?" she cried. "I don't know the rules to either game and even if I did, what fun is it to play with myself? If only Automated Alice were here! She would certainly know the rules to both the games. In fact, Automated Alice would know the rules so well, she would beat me in every single game! And I couldn't be doing with *that* at all! But still, it would be nice to have somebody to talk to. And also something to eat!"

Just then the key turned again in the lock and the door to the cell banged open. Inspector Jack Russell stepped into the room, carrying a plate of food. "I thought you might be hungry, Alice," he growled, setting the plate down on her bed.

"I am hungry," stated Alice, "but I shan't be eating that!" (It was a plateful of boiled radishes!)

"Very well," Jack Russell replied, "I shall take it away then."

"Where is Captain Ramshackle?" Alice asked.

"The badgerman is being questioned by the Over Assistant at this very moment, and the Lady of Snakes will be interrogating you presently."

"But I'm innocent, I tell you!"

"That's for the serpents to decide; meanwhile, I'm giving you a cell-companion . . ."

A slug was then dogmanhandled into Alice's cell. A rather large slug, at that! And the door clanged shut on them both. Imagine, Alice the sweet girl and a *greasily enormous slug* shut up tightly in a mere *pigeonhole* of a space? (Although, truth be known, even a pigeon would find that space rather too encroaching for comfort, let alone a young girl and a giant slug!) The slug wasn't just a slug, of course; he was also a man—a manslug. He was dressed in a suit of silky, shiny cloth, with a jacket and tie and trousers of glitter. On his black and glutinous head rested a large twirled hat of spirals, below which his pair of twitching horns moved slowly through the dank air. In his human hands he held a golden trumpet of finely polished brass.

"Who are you?" asked Alice, nervously.

"I . . . am . . . Long . . . Distance . . . Davis . . ." the slugman sluggishly replied, putting an age between each word. "And . . . who . . . are . . . you?"

"I'm Alice," replied Alice, "and you're a slug!"

"I . . . am . . . not . . . a . . . slug . . ." Long Distance Davis replied, just as slowly as before. "I . . . am . . . a . . . snail . . ."

"So where is your shell?" (Alice knew just enough about *gas-*

tropodology to understand that a snail had a shell, whereas a slug did not.)

"Wherever . . . I . . . lay . . . my . . . hat . . . is . . . my . . . shell . . ." With this utterance the snailman lay down on the dirt floor and then started to *smooth* his body into his hat. Around and around the spirals he went, until he had almost vanished; in fact, only his golden trumpet remained in sight. "Please don't go home to your shell, Mister Snailman!" Alice pleaded. "Please talk to me."

"What's . . . to . . . talk . . . about?" Long Distance Davis slovenly replied, from within the depths of his shell hat. "I . . . am . . . under . . . my . . . hat . . . and . . . also . . . under . . . arrest . . ."

"For what crime?" asked Alice.

"For . . . the . . . crime . . . of . . . playing . . . music . . ."

"Is it a crime to play music in the future?"

"I . . . was . . . playing . . . too . . . slowly . . ."

"I'm getting awfully confused, Mister Snailman; why should *slowness* be against the law?"

"The . . . Civil . . . Serpents . . . hate . . . waiting . . ."

"And what is it exactly that you're waiting for?" demanded Alice.

"I'm . . . waiting . . . for . . . the . . . next . . . note . . . to . . . escape . . . from . . . my . . . trumpet."

"Will you play me a tune right now, Mister Long Distance?" asked Alice, politely. "It would surely pass the time."

"I . . . shall . . . play . . . you . . . my . . . latest . . . composition . . ." Upon these torpid words the snailman slid completely free of his shell, so that it once again resembled a hat. "This . . . tune

. . . is . . . entitled . . . 'Miles . . . Behind' . . ." He then raised his shining trumpet to his greasy lips and blew out a single note:

"*Parp!*" went the trumpet. Long Distance Davis then lowered the instrument.

"Is that it?" asked Alice (having noticed that a jigsaw piece rested in the bell of the trumpet).

"That . . . is . . . the . . . beginning . . . of . . . the . . . piece . . ." Long Distance drawled.

"But why are you talking so slowly, Mister Snailman?" asked Alice (stealing the jigsaw piece from the snailman's trumpet whilst he was looking off into the far distance). "Aren't you very good at English?"

"I . . . don't . . . speak . . . Anguish . . ."

"I didn't say Anguish, I said English."

"Well . . . it . . . certainly . . . seems . . . like . . . you're . . . very . . . anguished . . ."

"What language *do* you speak then?" Alice was becoming quite exasperated at the snailman's sluggishness. (Or should that be snailiness? I can't make my mind up, can you?)

"I . . . speak . . . in . . . Languish . . ." the snailman eventually replied.

"And what is Languish?" asked Alice.

"Languish . . . is . . . the . . . lazy . . . language . . ."

The snailman then raised his trumpet to his lips and once again blew into it, fully two notes this time. (During this musical passage Alice managed a quick glance at her latest jigsaw piece; it showed only a black and greasy patch of wet skin. Alice knew that the piece was for the snail missing from her gastropod house at London Zoo. She silently slipped it into her pinafore pocket.)

"*Parp, parp!*" went the trumpet, before it was lowered once again.

"Is this still the tune called 'Miles Behind'?" Alice asked.

"Miles . . . and . . . miles . . . behind . . ."

"This must be why they call you Long Distance Davis, because you take so very long to do hardly anything at all!"

"This . . . *is* . . . why . . . they . . . call . . . me . . . Long . . . Distance . . . Davis . . ."

"Ridiculousness!" cried Alice, having completely lost her patience. "Here I am talking to a snailman who can't even finish a sentence properly, when I have so very much to do! I have so much to *find!*"

"Alice . . . you . . . must . . . play . . . it . . . cool . . ."

"But I'm not playing anything!" Alice cried. "And how can I be *cool,* when I'm pressed up tight against a warm and wet giant of a snailman in a tiny cell?"

"Cool . . . is . . . as . . . cool . . . does . . ."

"And what does cool do?"

"Cool . . . is . . . the . . . art . . . of . . . waiting . . ."

"Do you have anything to eat?" Alice asked then (having felt a wanting in her empty stomach, and also a wanting to change the subject). "Because I have grown mightily tired of waiting!"

"I . . . have . . . head . . . food . . ." replied Long Distance Davis, reaching into the bell end of his trumpet to produce a small velvet sack. This he slowly proceeded to unwrap: within its folds lay a silver jar, on which the words SWALLOW US were beautifully scripted in gold leaf. Long Distance Davis unscrewed the lid of the jar and then offered the contents to Alice. Alice took just one look at the contents and then reeled back, quite *bilious* at what she saw there. "You're offering me *worms* to eat!" she cried.

"These . . . are . . . not . . . worms . . ." Long Distance drawled. "These . . . are . . . wurms . . ."

"These are *wurms!*" Alice cried yet again, adding the U. "Won't they make me go crazy?"

"They . . . will . . . fulfil . . . your . . . need . . ."

"Very well then," Alice said (but only because she was so very hungry), "but you first."

With his untrumpeted hand, Long Distance Davis reached into the jar to bring up a wriggling, living specimen: this wurm he shovelled into his mouth. He then raised his trumpet to his lips to blow three more notes of the tune called "Miles Behind":

"*Parp, parp, parp!*" went the trumpet.

Long Distance Davis then scooped up another greasy wurm from the jar: "Your . . . turn . . . Alice . . ." he meandered, "please . . . take . . . a . . . little . . . trip . . . with . . . me . . ."

Alice decided that she had very little choice anyway, if she wanted to eat: so she allowed Long Distance Davis to slither the wurm into her mouth.

Oh my goodness! The wurm was *slippering* its way down her throat! Alice fell back on to the bed in a falling faint.

And then everything went very slipperty-jipper indeed . . .

OXO

Alice is now floating along a long snake of water, through a slowly turning world of golden-afternoon colours. It takes her an age to realise that she is no longer inside the prison cell; it takes her an age and a half to realise that she is now lazily reclining in a small rowing boat. Her two sisters, Lorina and Edith, are aboard the boat with her, as is her friend, the kind Mister Dodgson. It takes Alice *two whole ages* to realise that Mister Dodgson is now telling fanciful stories to the three little maidens.

"Tell us more, Mister Dodgson!" shrieks Edith at Alice's left. "Tell us more! More, more, *more!*"

"But my dearest girls . . ." breathes Mister Dodgson, "the well of fancy has run quite dry, how can I *possibly* continue?"

"Oh but you *must* continue!" cries Alice from the boat's bed.

"The rest next time—" the story-teller tries in vain.

"It *is* next time!" the happy voices squeal as one.

"Oh very well then, if you insist . . ."

The boat now drifts aground at the small village of Godstow on the Thames' bank, and the four friends disembark to take a picnic underneath a spreading elm tree: and here, between bites at a boiled ham sandwich (with not a single radish to be seen anywhere!), Mister Dodgson continues with his tale of *Alice's Adventures Underground.* The three sisters are so enraptured by his tale that Alice doesn't realise, until it's far, far too late, that a worm has wriggled its way into her sandwich: she takes a bite of ham, and also a bite of worm!

Alice recoils from the taste, and spits the offending morsel out of her mouth! "Alice, my dearest," whispers Mister

Dodgson, "you do know that little girls shouldn't waste their food in such a manner?"

"But it's got a worm in it!" protests Alice, still spitting. "And I fear that I've swallowed more than half of it, already!" Alice spits and spits, and spits and spits and spits! The soil is by now entirely covered in spume, and Alice notices that a whole knotted *wrigglesome* of worms is crawling over the picnic cloth! The worms are unfolding themselves upwards to grab at Alice's ankles, which is mightily strange, but the strangest thing of all is that Alice feels more than happy to allow the worms to slither around her flesh, even though they are dragging her below the very soil of England! Alice's three picnicking companions seem to be oblivious to her plight; they carry on eating and drinking and telling tales, as though nothing out of the ordinary is happening! And Alice is now happy to see that Whippoorwill the parrot is flying over the elm trees towards her. "Come to me, my sweet bird of youth," Alice cries out. "Come and join me in the swim of these worms: we could surrender to the loopiness together. Wouldn't that be nice, Whippoorwill?" Alice is by this time half-sunk into the soil, and the worms are twisting around her with a thousand slitherings. Alice feels wonderful, especially when Whippoorwill flies down to perch upon her outstretched hand. "There, there, my long-lost," Alice breathes softly, stroking at the feathers, "at last you've come home to me."

"Who is it, Alice," the parrot riddles, "that contains only the half of the whole?"

"Why the answer is *me,* of course, Whippoorwill," answers

Alice, quite confidently, "because there's only a half of my whole remaining above this worm hole: and I'm very much looking forward to sinking all the way down!" At which Alice starts to giggle and wriggle about in order to drown herself in the worm bath.

"Right answer, Alice!" squawks back Whippoorwill, "but for all the wrong reasons. Think again and quickly, Alice. Before you sink down too deeply."

"But the worms have such a warmthiness about them, dearest Whippoorwill," says Alice, ever-so-happily. "I've never felt so much at home . . ."

"Alice, listen to me clearly," says Whippoorwill in a surprisingly human voice. "These are not worms that you're drowning in, these are wurms; worms with a U in the name: the name that stands for *wisdom-undoing-randomised-mechanism*, as you well have learned. The wurms just want you to go crazy, and to remain in the future forever."

"What in the earth are you talking about, Whippoorwill?" asks Alice, up to her shoulders in the soil. "And what is so very wrong with going crazy?"

"Alice, you will never get home at this rate," squawks the parrot. "You will be forever lost in time."

"But I *am* home," replies Alice, sternly, and trying to stamp her foot. "And if being home is the same as being lost, well then, I shall want to be gratefully lost forever!"

"I'm trying my squawking best to lead you back to the past," replies Whippoorwill. "Only by following me will you get home in time for your writing lesson."

"Lessons! *Pooh* to lessons! Oh dear, I said a naughty! Well I don't care. I want to be naughty! I like it here, really. Let me sink, my feathery friend . . ." And Alice does sink then, deeper and deeper.

"Very well," beaks the parrot. "I shall now leave you to the wurms. Let the crazies swallow you. You obviously want to be a pretty fool." And with that utterance the parrot flies off into the far distance and Alice is suddenly alone again: suddenly alone with only the wurms of warmth to nuzzle at her cheekbones. Mister Dodgson and her sisters, Lorina and Edith; they have all vanished quite away. And Alice *does* feel like she is being swallowed, all of a sudden. At this moment Alice notices *something else again* nudging into the corner of her vision. She has a real job turning her head around in the wurms, but somehow she does. And this is what she sees: a large grandfather clock has appeared on the grass, a few yards away from Alice's sinking visage. The clock's hands are applauding the imminent arrival of two o'clock. And then the clock's mouth dings a double dong: it's two o'clock in Wurmland and out of the clock's body come bouncing three large and very bulbous black dots!

"Oh dear!" Alice murmurs to herself. "Here I am being eaten alive by the crazy wurms, without a hope of escape; and the time is two o'clock! I'm late for my lesson! And if I'm not mistaken, that trio of large, black and angry-looking bubbles racing towards me is an Ellipsis! Oh, what a horrible creature an Ellipsis is! Maybe I should escape from this wurmy world. But however can I manage it?" The wurms were now nudging against Alice's nostrils! "I must try to think of a plan!" she mumbled. "Now let me see . . . the wurm came into my body through my mouth; how can I now get rid of that wrigglesome wanderer? Only by the never passage, I fear."

(The never passage is of course the nether passage: the passage that can never be written about. But if my dearest Alice can only escape the world of the wurms by this terrible evacuation, then so be it, for I must give my writing to the young girl's future.)

By this time (thanks to my hesitation in the story's telling) the three dots of the Ellipsis monster are gathering around Alice's head in a squelchy triangle of bubbles.

"My name is Dot," the first bubble says.

"My name is also Dot," the second bubble says.

"My name is also and also Dot," the third bubble says. The trio of bubbles move in on Alice, ever closer, ever closer . . .

Alice feels herself being engulfed by the wurms and the Dots, and very terrified she is by the stifling presence of these two engulfers; so very terrified that she actually excretes the wurm.

(May I by the way explain that the rather naughty word called *excrete* comes from the Latin for *separate* and *discharge,* and if a word comes from the Latin, it surely cannot be that naughty? Suffice it to say politely that Alice did separate and discharge the wurm from her body, through the never passage . . .)

○○○

And through this passage Alice arrived back in her tiny cell below the police station. Long Distance Davis was curled up, snail-like, in his shell of a hat on the dirt floor, still travelling in the wurm's dream. Alice shook her head from side to side twenty-seven-and-a-half times, in order to dispel the remnants of the wurminess, and then she announced sternly to herself, "Whippoorwill was right: I have been a pretty fool up to now. I have allowed myself to be carried along by strangers through this future world. From now on, I shall carry myself! I shall find my *own way* back to Great Aunt Ermintrude's house."

Alice noticed the jigsaw pieces scattered on the floor. She picked them up carefully, added the snail piece from her pocket, and rearranged all six of them around the stolen feather from Whippoorwill. It was then that she found the real answer to Whippoorwill's last riddle: Who is it that contains only the half of the whole? Alice realised that the parrot had said *hole,* and not *whole.* Who is it that contains only the half of the hole? That was the question. Alice now knew that the hole that Whippoorwill had riddled about was the hole in her jigsaw of London Zoo, or rather, the twelve holes that the missing pieces were waiting to fill.

"Why, this whole future I'm trapped within," Alice cried out loud, "is nothing more than a jigsaw of the past. If I can gather together all of the lost pieces, perhaps I will find my way back through the hole in time!" She then counted the pieces she had already collected: the termite piece, the badger piece, the snake, the chicken, the zebra and the snail piece. "That makes six pieces," she added to herself. "I have six more to find, because twelve pieces were missing from my long-ago jigsaw. I *did* give the right answer to Whippoorwill's riddle, but for all the wrong reasons. I am the girl that contains only the half of the hole."

Alice tried her best to remember the six pieces she was still missing: "There was a spider from the spider house, and a cat from the cat house, but they are both in the possession of the police! And what about the other four pieces? There was a fish missing from the aquarium, I'm sure, and also a crow from the aviary, and a parrot, I believe. Why, that piece must represent Whippoorwill! I must surely catch him so that I can arrive back in time for my writing lesson. And I still don't know the correct usage for an ellipsis, even though a three-dotted monster wanted to eat me in Wurmland! But there was one other jigsaw piece missing as well. Now then, what was it? Oh bother, I simply cannot recall it, no matter how hard I try! And anyway, however shall I find those jigsawed creatures while I am languishing in jail? And what about Celia? I must also find my Automated Alice. And I expect I must also try to find out who the real Jigsaw Murderer is, in order to prove my innocence! Oh dear! I've got so many things to find. I shall never get home!"

Just then the door to the cell opened. It was Inspector Jack Russell, popping his furry head in. "Alice," he barked, "please come with me and quickly! Our Lady of the Snakes is now ready for you. Your conviction will play a vigorous role in her election campaign."

Alice was quite fearful of meeting such a high-up Civil Serpent, but really she had no choice at all. Indeed, she had less than a second's chance to pat Long Distance's sleeping shell-shape, and to gather up all the jigsaw pieces and the parrot's feather, before Jack Russell whiskered her out of the cell. Down a long twisting of corridors they travelled, and up an ever-increasing series of stairways. Alice became disorientated yet again. "Why, the future is so full of mazes," she said to herself, "it's a wonder anybody can get anywhere!"

Presently she was led through a door marked CHAMBER OF INTERROGATION, into a room of mirrors. "Wait here," Jack Russell growled at her. "The Over Assistant will be along shortly to question you." He left the room, banging the mirrored door shut behind him. Alice looked all around in order to find an escape, but the mirrored walls repeated her image time and time again, until Alice was quite lost in her reflections. There was an infinitude of Alices in the room!

"This is really all too much!" she reflected to herself, reflected to herself, reflected to herself, reflected to herself, reflected to herself (*ad infinitum*). "I shall never find my true self in this room of mirrors."

Just then, a thousand elusive images of Whippoorwill started to dance around the room!

"Oh dear!" cried Alice, as she flickered here and there trying to catch even one of the thousand feathery images. "How shall I know which is the real Whippoorwill?" she cried, "and which the unreal? And in any case, I wonder what the collective noun for parrots is?"

"The collective noun," answered a croaky voice from out of nowhere, "is a pandemonium of parrots."

"Who said that?" asked Alice in surprise.

"Celia said it," answered the voice of a thousand parrots, as one of Alice's reflections peeled itself free from the mirrors.

"Is that really you, Celia?" asked Alice of the wayward reflection.

The reflection reflected, ".uoy eucser ot gniyrt m'I .aileC yllaer si siht ,seY" And the reflection vanished once more into

a merely mirrored image, taking all the reflections of Whippoorwill with it.

One of the mirrors then opened, and a snakewoman came slithering forwards from the reflection of the reflection of a snakewoman, whose curling body was somehow arranged into a vaguely human shape.

Alice was quite taken aback. "What do you want of me?" she asked of the snakewoman. "Are you an adder?"

"I am a Subtracter," replied the snakewoman. "My name is Mrs Minus. I am the prime candidate for imminent election to the position of New Supreme Serpent."

"What happened to the *old* Supreme Serpent?" asked Alice.

"He died from too much addition. I, on the other fork, subtract the crimes of this world: the jigsaw murder of a spiderboy, for instance . . ."

"But, you must understand, I was in the year 1860 when the spiderboy was killed!"

"That is not nearly good enough, my little suspect!" Mrs Minus replied, wrapping a strangulation of her thick coils around Alice's body. "Your alibi smells of high wantonness. You have already admitted to the ownership of the murderous jigsaw pieces. I am hereby charging you with Probable Involvement in the crime of murder. Captain Ramshackle is the killer of the spiderboy and the catgirl; he wants nothing more than to bring chaos to the world, and *you,* troublesome Alice, are the badgerman's helper in this endeavour. You shall be executed for this." Mrs Minus then produced an evil-looking pistol from a pocket in her skin. She pointed it at Alice . . .

"But I'm innocent!" squealed Alice. ("Innocent . . . innocent . . . innocent . . ." reflected the thousand mirrors, all to no avail: Mrs Minus had every single image of Alice wrapped in her tightening coils.) At which thankful moment Inspector Jack Russell came bursting into the room.

"Has my election campaign mascot arrived, Inspector?" asked the snakewoman.

"Not yet, Our Lady of Slitherness," replied Inspector Jack, nervously, "but I have to report that there has been an escape from the cells . . ."

"Who has escaped, Inspector Russell?"

"Captain Ramshackle."

"Captain Ramshackle! You puppified fool!"

Mrs Minus released Alice in order to wrap her slinky knots around Jack Russell's body. A pack of wild policedogmen came howling by, and Mrs Minus and Inspector Jack Russell swiftly joined them in the search for Captain Ramshackle. Alice peeked out of the cell and looked along the corridor. In the long distance she saw Long Distance Davis escaping (at quite a pace for a snail!). On the other side of the corridor rested another door. This one was marked with the number forty-five and the words ROOM OF EVIDENCE, and it was through this forty-fived door that Alice slipped, to escape from the police.

VII

THE STROKE

OF NOON

THE

Room of Evidence was freezing cold, and Alice was shivering as soon as she closed the door behind her. She hugged her red pinafore around herself (checking her pockets to be sure that the six jigsaw pieces and the feather were still safe) and ventured forth into the coldness.

The Room of Evidence was lined with cabinets wall to wall, and filled up with large tables, all of which were empty except for one, on which lay a white sheet covering a lumpy shape. Alice noticed that a notice attached to the sheet was labelled with a label that read WHISKERS MACDUFF. Alice slowly lifted up the sheet . . .

Alice screamed then as she had never screamed before! "Upon my kittens!" was her strangled cry. She backed away from the table in a rush, fell over her own legs, and ended up in a heap of herself on the floor!

The reason for Alice's discomfort was that, upon lifting the sheet, she had uncovered the dead and rearranged body of the catgirl, Whiskers Macduff. Alice had never seen anything dead before, and the sight of such a thing made her go all wobbly. "I must be a strong young girl!" she was now saying to herself as she got back to her feet. "I must grow myself up!" Alice forced herself to look at the body. The catgirl's face was covered in a fine gingery fur from which a pair of startled human eyes were staring, lifelessly. The head of the catgirl was melded to the juncture between her furry legs; her whiskers were sprouting from her thighs; her hind paws were growing out of her gingery chest. Her furry ears were planted upon each of her elbows (if cats have elbows, that is; Alice wasn't sure). And clipped with a brass safety pin to the catgirl's left ear was a small linen bag. Alice, being curious, searched inside the bag and found a piece from a wooden jigsaw. She quite rightly decided to keep the jigsaw piece, which illustrated the golden eye of a wildcat. This feline fragment she added to the collection in her pocket. She had now collected seven pieces of the puzzle. Alice was more than half-way home!

But it was so cold in that freezing room that Alice's tears were forming icicles, and she decided to find a way out. "I certainly can't escape through the door I came in by," she shivered to herself; "those horrible policedogmen might still be lingering there. But there seems to be no other doorway! Whatever shall I do now?" She was still looking all around when the only door opened and a very tired-looking, old bloodhoundman came lolloping in! He was dressed in a crisply clean and spotless white gown and his long face hung down with a hangdog expression, complete with briefcase eyes, a dripping wet nose and a long and lollingly pink tongue. This creature sniffed at the air with a gruff huff, twice times, and then lowly growled, "Who in the iciness are you?"

"I'm icy Alice," replied Alice, "and who are you?"

"My name is Doctor Sniffer," the bloodhound replied sniffingly. "I am the Chief Examiner of Corpses. What are you doing standing so close to my next job of work? And why is the body uncovered?"

"I was only being curious," answered Alice, quite truthfully.

"Curiosity killed the cat," growled Sniffer, stepping forwards to examine the catgirl's corpse for tampering. "I trust you haven't been *too* curious?"

"Of course not," replied Alice (not so truthfully). "I was only trying to work out the reason for the catgirl's . . . that is to say . . . the reason why she had to die . . ."

"That's my job, young girl! And you're hindering my examination!"

Alice stepped back then and watched with trepidation as Doctor Sniffer snipped some locks of ginger fur from the body of Whiskers Macduff. These locks he then examined under a microscope. (Luckily he never bothered to examine the contents of the small linen bag.) "This is such a mysterious case," Sniffer gruffed after a few moments. "We cannot find out exactly how the victims died, only that their bodies are in some way strangely jigsawed. The prime suspect is one Captain Ramshackle, but he seems to have escaped us. Confound it! But no matter: all I have to do is find some traces of badger fur on the body." Sniffer was twiddling at the knurled knob of his microscope as he said these words.

"I do not believe that Captain Ramshackle is the culprit," stated Alice.

Doctor Sniffer raised up his luggagey eyes from the microscope. "That is for me to decide, young girl! Am I not, after all, the Chief Examiner of Corpses?"

"You most certainly are the Chiefest Examiner of Corpses," replied Alice, before adding, "Could you therefore please tell me where the first victim of the Jigsaw Murderer might be?"

"The spiderboy called Quentin Tarantula has long since passed through my paws, I'm afraid; his body has been buried."

"And what would have happened to any clues found on his body?"

"That now belongs to the Civil Serpents: the Big Snakes are making their own examination of the clues."

"So the spiderboy's jigsaw piece must be inside the Town Hall?"

"Exactly so!" answered Doctor Sniffer, "and quite rightly: deep, down below the Town Hall."

"Oh dear," sighed Alice to herself. "I shall have a hard time finding it then."

"And may I ask what you are doing," Sniffer sniffed, "in my Room of Evidence?"

"I'm looking for a way out," replied Alice, calmly.

"There are only two ways out of this room: the first is through the front door." Sniffer pointed with a limp paw towards the door that Alice had entered by.

"And where is the second way out?" asked Alice (rather *too* eagerly).

"Through this door here, of course," Sniffer answered, tapping with his claws on an iron trapdoor set in the floor of the Room of Evidence. "This is where I shovel the corpses when I've finished my examination." Sniffer lifted up the trapdoor to reveal a gaping hole in the floor. "This is the only other way out of the room," he growled at Alice. "This orifice leads

directly to the cemetery, but you have to be officially dead to descend that far."

"But I *am* officially dead!" squealed Alice, triumphantly (and rather desperate to make her escape from the Room of Evidence).

"You look very much alive to me," breathed Sniffer.

"I was born in 1852! Which means that I'm one hundred and forty-six years old! Surely nobody can be that old, Doctor Sniffer?"

"You should certainly be extremely dead by now, Alice: but can you prove your age to me? Have you your birth certificate, for instance?"

"I'm afraid not," Alice replied, "but I have this ..." She pulled Whippoorwill's lost feather from her pinafore pocket.

"Well, let me investigate it," growled Sniffer, taking the feather from Alice's hand, and then placing it under his microscope. "But this is preposterous!" he then barked, lifting his baggy eye from the lens. "According to my forensic examination, this feather comes from a parrot that was alive in 1860! Either you're an obsessive collector of Nineteenth Century Avarian Accessories, or else you should really have died a long, long time ago."

"*Now* will you believe me, Doctor Sniffer?"

"But then you must be the very ghost of a girl!"

Alice grabbed the feather from the microscope and then said, "I do feel like the ghost of a girl, actually. I feel like I'm neither here nor there, or anywhere at all, come to think of it!"

"My poor little girl, how very sad that must be." A pair of long, droopy tears were falling from the Doctor's baggy eyes.

"Will you please deliver me to the cemetery, Doctor Sniffer," Alice pleaded, "where I can find my true home."

"Oh very well then! But quickly, child, before the Civil Serpents find me out for doing such a strangeness." Doctor Sniffer then shovelled Alice through the gulping hole in the floor.

And so it was that Alice went sliding down a long chute of darkness.

Through darknesses and darknesses and darknesses, Alice slid; until, eventually, she slid out of the nether end of the chute and straight into a wooden cart that was fixed to the hindquar-

ters of a beastly black mechanical auto-horse. She landed on
the top of a mound of large, filled sacks that squelched dreadfully under her weight. Alice didn't want to consider what was
inside those sacks, because the smell rising from their contents
was quite noxifying! She decided to climb out of the cart, and
she would have done exactly that, had not the auto-horse then
commenced to gallop off along the road at a terrifying pace,
and without any need at all for a driver!

Within five-and-a-half rickety seconds or so Alice was being
driven around a place called Albert Square, where the Town
Hall of Manchester magnificently loomed. "I do believe this
auto-horse is not a horse at all," she said to herself. "This auto-
horse is an auto-hearse! I don't think I want to be delivered to
the cemetery just yet!" Alice jumped out of the hearse and cart
whilst it was still travelling along at speed. She did slightly
scrape her right knee upon landing, but this was a small price
to pay for escaping a far-too-early visit to the cemetery!
Unfortunately there was a larger price to pay: without her
knowledge, Whippoorwill's green-and-yellow feather had
escaped her pocket during the fall.

The auto-hearse galloped off around the next corner, leaving the still-alive-Alice in Albert Square. It had stopped raining
by now and the square was packed with people enjoying the
lunch-timing sunshine. These weren't the kind of people that
Alice was used to, of course, because all of them seemed to
have an animalised part to their natures. There were several
Squirrelmen in the square; there were also Ostrichmen in the
square. There were also Lama and Goat and Beetle and Cow

and Dog and Snake and Trout and Gorilla and Antelope and Sparrow and Puma and Turkey and even Jellyfish-men and -women in the square. And all of these mix-ups were feeding their faces with greasy meat pies and slivers of fried potato!

There were also several even stranger creatures that Alice encountered in Albert Square: people jigsawed together with objects. Pianogirls, for instance, and Soapboys, Curtaingirls and Wardrobing kids. "Why, everything except for the kitchen sink seems to have become a quite acceptable part of the human body!" Alice was only just thinking this random thought, when what should she notice gurgling through the

crowd but a man with a kitchen sink in place of a head! This sunken creature dribbled past Alice, stuffing a sandwich into his plug-hole. Alice ran away as fast as she could! (Which wasn't hardly fast enough at all, because of the closely knitted and knotted nature of the crowd.) Alice had to fairly iron her way between birdcaging girls and brief-casing boys and the mutated spectaclemen joined at the topiary to newspapering people of bicycle and bone! Alice felt ever so

lonely, pushing her way through that crowd of strangely strange strangers, especially when they all seemed to press against her so, and to stare at her so, and to whisper abusive words at her, just so!

As though Alice herself was the strange one!

"The disease that's called Newmonia seems to be troubling

nearly everything!" Alice sighed to herself. "So many of these creatures resemble Pablo Ogden's sculptures, and yet they seem to be perfectly real rather than perfectly automated. I suppose I must only do my best to ignore the stares and the whispers, and to continue my search for Whippoorwill and Celia and the five remaining jigsaw pieces. But the police will be searching for Captain Ramshackle; and they will also be searching for me!"

Indeed, Alice did then notice a policedogman growling at the edges of the crowd, so she immediately pushed her way deeper into the tumult of strangeness, hoping to find a breathing space there. But the crowd pushed and brushed and tushed against her so much that Alice was eventually squashed up against a stone statue in the centre of Albert Square. Alice noticed that it was carved into the exact resemblance of Albert Francis Charles Augustus Emmanuel of Saxe-Coburg-Gotha: in other words, Prince Albert, the consort of Queen Victoria of Great Britain. "So this is why they call this place Albert Square," Alice realised. "Prince Albert must have died a long, long time ago, just like *I* must have died a long, long time ago; after all, we do share the same first syllabub." (A syllabub is, of course, a dessert made from cream beaten with sugar, wine and lemon juice; I really do think that Alice meant to say syllable!) "Alice and Albert," Alice continued to herself; "maybe I was correct when I pretended to Doctor Sniffer that I was dead . . ."

Alice was so full of sadness at her own demise. "Am I dead, or am I not dead?" she wondered, with a small cry. "And when is a garden not a garden? And is a bean here, or is a bean not here?" Alice was becoming ever so confused with her own beanness.

But Alice quickly shrugged off her confusion, so determined was she to find her way out of this puzzle. She started marching once again through the clinging crowd until she arrived at the Town Hall's grand entrance. Here she encountered a liveried doormandog—half a man, half a guard dog—who demanded to know her name and her business. "My name is Alice," Alice replied, "and my business is to retrieve a spidery jigsaw piece that rightfully belongs to me. I believe that the Civil Serpents are keeping it inside the Town Hall."

"I'm afraid I cannot allow you entrance," the doormandog growled back. "That would be more than my bone's worth. You have no business here!" And the doormandog growled so fiercely then that Alice was forced to run backwards into the crowd of Newmonia sufferers, through which a whole pack of policemandogs were now snuffling, asking questions of everybody. Alice decided to hide herself behind a rather colourful umbrella woman. "I really am getting nowhere at all," she cried, once hidden. "The future seems to be so completely against me; how can I possibly hope to presently find my past?" Alice then looked up towards the large and impressive clock face that adorned the Town Hall's tower; the time was rushing towards noon. "Oh dear!" Alice added and subtracted to herself. "I must have spent simply *hours* in the police cell! It's coming up to exactly twelve, and in nearly exactly two hours' time and also nearly exactly one hundred and thirty-eight years ago I should have been present at my writing lesson with Great Aunt Ermintrude!"

Alice saw then that a single green-and-yellow feather was floating above the Square. "Why, that looks like one of Whippoorwill's feathers," she cried. "Maybe the whole parrot himself is flying around this square somewhere? I must look out for him!" And Alice did look out for Whippoorwill, but only the single feather of him was to be seen, floating along on a slight breeze. "Whippoorwill!" cried Alice to the single feather (having nothing further to cry to), "if you keep on losing feathers at this rate, why, very soon you will not be able to fly at all!" She then dug deep into her pinafore pocket for *her* feather. Of course, she found only the seven jigsaw pieces. "Oh flutterings!" Alice howled. "That's my feather floating up there! I must have dropped it getting out of the auto-hearse!" Alice reached up into the air to recapture the feather, but no matter how high she reached, she could never quite reach it.

And just as Alice was reaching her very highest high in order to grab at Whippoorwill's escaping feather, the Town Hall clock started to slowly ding-dong its clanging song of middaying chimes. At the very first of the chimes, Alice felt a soft hand softly stroking at her shoulder. She thought that it must be the paw of a policedogman, come to rearrest her, and she pushed it away, but when she eventually spun around to view the stroker, imagine her surprise to find a normal man waiting for her there. This normal man was utterly and only a normal man—not a single trace of animality—and he was jacketed in a deep and blue velvety suit, complete with a deep and blue and peaked and velvety cap. Over his left shoulder lay the straps of a deep and blue and velvety bag. Everything about him was velvety!

"Who are you?" asked Alice.

"They call me Zenith O'Clock," responded the normal man.

"Who do?"

"*Time* calls me Zenith O'Clock, because I was born upon this very minute exactly thirty-eight years ago, when the sun was at its veritable height." Zenith reached up to point at the Town Hall clock (which was ever-so-slowly chiming its way through the second of its dozen ding-dongs).

"It's your birthday?" Alice cried.

"It is indeed the anniversary of my birth."

"Many happy returns!"

"I sincerely hope never to return to this day."

"Why ever not?"

"This is a dreadful day for me, a dreadful day, I tell you! And very sad I am to be living it. Your name is Alice, isn't it? Your full name is Alice Pleasance Liddell?"

"My full name *is* Alice Pleasance Liddell. But how in the world did you know that?"

"I've seen you before, but only in books."

"Only in books?" asked Alice.

"Only in books, as you say. Only! Books can never be only; they can only be always. Oh, but all this talk of books is bringing back my sadness!"

"But it's your birthday, Mister O'Clock!" cried Alice; "upon this day you should only be happy!"

"I cannot be happy," Zenith replied, "because I'm suffering from a terrible disease."

"But you look perfectly healthy to me," Alice responded. "I'm so glad to have met another purely human being. Surely you can't be suffering from the Newmonia?"

"I have a more deadly disease: I'm infested with the Crickets, you see."

"You're infested with cricket?" misheard Alice. "The game with a bat, a ball, three stumps and an umpire?"

"Crickets, I said! Not cricket! Cricket in the plural and with a capital C: that ravenous cloud of reviewing insects. I'm a writer, you see."

"And what do you write, Mister O'Clock? Timetables?" (Alice was quite pleased with her joke.)

"No, no," replied Zenith. "I have found it impossible to time a table, although I once tried. A table is much too wooden to make more than a breath of a move, once every nine hours: except at dinnertime, when it may well make a sudden run for the kitchen."

"So what do you write?" insisted Alice. "Fiction or non-fiction?"

"I write neither fiction nor non-fiction. Rather I write Friction."

"And what is Friction, pray?"

"I write in the language called Frictional. I'm a writer of Wrongs."

"Whatever's a Wrong?"

"A Wrong is a book that the crickets don't consider to be right, preferring their stories to be told in Simpleton rather than Frictional. They rub their dry wings together, these crickets, making a terrible response to my work in the noisepapers."

"But what's so terrible about your Wrongs?" asked Alice.

"Well, I've written two Wrongs up to now: the first was called *Shurt,* and the second was called *Solumn.* And the crickets hated both of them. This is why I'm so sad upon my birthday."

"Do you always spell your book-titles with too many U's in them?"

"I can't help it, I'm afraid. I can't help going wrong. Shall I read you a little passage from one of my books?"

"If you wish," replied Alice.

Zenith then reached into his velvety bag, to pull out a copy of the book called *Shurt.* It had a bright azure cover, decorated with an illuminated pair of yellow shirts. Zenith shuffled through the pages of his book until he found the passage he was looking for. "This is a love poem called 'Nothing Rhymes With Orange.' Are you ready for it, Alice?"

"I hope so: except that *nothing* doesn't rhyme at all with *orange*."

"Excellent! Then I'll begin . . ."

And this is the poem that Zenith began:

> *"Nothing can rhyme with an orange*
> *Except the pocket on a kilt,*
> *When a sporran is misspelled*
> *To a sporrange with a lilt."*

"What do you think of it so far, Alice?" Zenith asked.

"Well," Alice answered hesitantly, "you told me it was going to be a love poem, but I can't find any trace of love in the words."

"But that was only the first verse."

"How many verses are there, all together?"

"Only two."

"Oh joy!" Alice said (quietly to herself).

And this is the poem that Zenith continued:

> *"An orange can rhyme with nothing!*
> *The people cry in ignorance:*
> *Forgetting in their ignorrange*
> *That words can be made to dance."*

Having finished his poem, Zenith looked at Alice with an expectant gaze. The crowd of Prince Albert's Square was closing in on Alice and she was feeling very uncomfortable, with

the crush and the request for yet another of her honest opin-
ions. "Well," she began, "I'm afraid I still can't see why you call
it a love poem."

"But I'm in love with language! Can't you see that?"

"Does this love allow you to make up words like sporrange
and ignorrange, just so you can make orange rhyme with
something rather than nothing?"

Zenith looked rather upset at this outburst of cricketing, and
Alice was beginning to regret having spoken her mind. "But
those words are my own creation!" spluttered Zenith. "They are
Frictional words: I conceived them; I gave birth to them! I *nur-
tured* those words so they'd grow up to be big and strong and
powerful; so that one day they could find themselves being
accepted into a Simpleton dictionary! That's my desire, you see,
Alice: I make play with old words, twice nightly—why, sometimes
even thrice nightly!—just so they can breed new words. But
you—especially you, Alice—you must understand my desire;
having been such a close friend of Charles Dodgson?"

"You know about Mister Dodgson?" exclaimed Alice.

"I know all about *you,* Alice," replied Zenith. "I've seen pictures of your likeness in the books called *Adventures in
Wonderland* and *Through the Looking-Glass.* Charles Dodgson
wrote them both about you."

"I know this already!" Alice explained, impatiently.

"But when Charles Dodgson wrote about you, he called himself Lewis Carroll: having decided, like myself, to hide behind
a *nom de plume,* which means a feather name."

"So you're not really called Zenith O'Clock?"

"Of course not! What a silly name that would be!"

"So what is your real name?"

"You want to know my *nom de real,* Alice? Now that would be telling. But what are you doing here in Manchester, Alice, and in 1998 of all ages?"

"I fell through a grandfather clock's workings," Alice replied. "And I need to get home in time for my two o'clock writing lesson."

"Maybe you should look up your history in the Central Library."

"But why should my history be in the library?" Alice demanded.

"Because you're famous in this age, Alice. The history of your life is contained in a book called *Reality and Realicey.*"

"Whatever does realicey mean?"

"Realicey is a special kind of reality: the world of the imagination, and it's so much more powerful than everyday existence! Witness your ability to discourse with me, Alice, all these many years after your real life! Maybe I should write my third book about you. I would call it *Through the Clock's Workings and What Alice Found There.*"

"But that's a silly title, Mister O'Clock! Because I've found hardly anything at all in my travels through the clock: I still have another five jigsaw pieces to find, and my parrot called Whippoorwill, and my doll called Celia, who's a kind of Automated Alice."

"Automated Alice . . . erm . . . that gives me a new idea . . . I will write a trequel!"

Alice wasn't sure how anybody could write with treacle: wouldn't the words come out all sticky? "If you really are such a clever writer, Mister O'Clock," she asked, "could you please tell me what an ellipsis is?"

"An ellipsis is the three dots that a writer uses to imply an omittance of words, a certain lingering doubt at the end of an unfinished sentence . . ."

"Oh thank you! I have found at least *one* of my lost objects!" And then Alice found another lost object, because a feather came floating down from the Square's air into her fingers. "This is a Whippoorwill feather!" Alice squealed.

"Whippoorwill?" said Zenith. "What a wonderful *nom de plume.* In my trequel, I will turn this feather into a tickling ticket for you."

"Why should I need a tickling ticket?" asked Alice.

"That's the only help I can give you, Alice; do you hear me? Or else the Coincidence Bureau will surely arrest me. Oh but I've just realised: perhaps I'm already writing the book called *Automated Alice,* and we two are merely characters within it?"

Alice wanted to ask what he meant, but just then, the Town Hall clock reached the twelfth of its slowed-down ding-dongs, and the writer's hand came down to stroke once again at Alice's pinafored shoulder. It was noon. It was that very softest of touches, the breath of friendship, amidst strangers . . . and then he was gone . . .

ALICE

LOOKS UP

HERSELF

HOW very sad Alice was to have lost hold of Mister O'Clock's normality, amidst the pressing concerns of the six-of-this and half-a-dozen-of-the-other crowd, this ever-changing throng that was pushing into her tender flesh from all sides. Pushing and pushing. In fact, pushing and pushing and *pushing!* Alice felt like she was being squashed flat by strangeness! But at least she knew what an ellipsis was, or at least she thought that she did. "If I can only find my way back home before two o'clock, 1860," she announced out loud to nobody in particular, "I could then finish my homework! But I must still find Whippoorwill and Celia before I can go home. Wherever can they have got to?" Alice looked all around the Square of Prince Albert, until her eyes were filled with tears. "Oh dear!" she spluttered. "I'm crying so much that the whole square seems to be filling up with water!"

Indeed, Albert Square was filling up with water, but it was only the tears of Heaven raining down once again. Alice felt rather sheepish when she realised that it was only the rain filling up the Square, and not her tears alone. (Have you ever seen a sheep in the rain? Well, that's exactly how Alice felt.) The crowd of animals, animates, animen, aniwomen and anioldiron were rushing out of the Square to escape the downpour, leaving Alice quite alone once again.

But not quite alone! Because, yes! there was Whippoorwill! He was fluttering above the Square, and making rather a bad job of the fluttering, because all the rainwater had drenched his wings. Alice quickly reached up to try and catch him; in fact, Alice didn't even need to try, the parrot was so bogged down with moisture: Alice captured him quite easily. "Whippoorwill!" she scolded, "look at the state you're in! Whatever will Great Aunt Ermintrude say when I get you home? You will come home with me now, won't you?"

To which the parrot made no reply at all except to look at her with a sideways eye and squawk out another riddle. "Who is it, Alice, that lives between an octopus's area and Ceylon's favourite stethoscope?"

"Well . . ." commenced Alice, "I almost know where the country called Ceylon is; I've seen it on a map of the world in the school room. I seem to remember that it is famous for growing tea-leaves, but I didn't know that the country had a favourite stethoscope. I didn't know that Ceylon had any stethoscopes at all, let alone a favourite one! And as to how much area an octopus covers: well, I suppose it all depends on how many of his eight legs he might have stretched out, or coiled. But really, Whippoorwill, what could possibly live between two such strange things?"

"Quickly, Alice!"

"Really, I can't make my mind up!"

"Can't make your mind up!" squawked Whippoorwill. "Try making your mind down!"

"I *can* make my mind up, sometimes at least," replied Alice, "but how can I possibly make my mind *down?* That doesn't seem right at all!"

"You must become more left than right, Alice," shrieked the parrot. "You must become more down than up! You must find the person that lives between an octopus's area and Ceylon's favourite stethoscope." And upon those wet and slippery words Whippoorwill managed to slip away from Alice's hands!

"Whippoorwill!" called out Alice. "Come back here, immediately!" But off he flew once again, vanishing into the skies of Manchester. "Oh, this is too, too much!" sulked Alice. "Why is Whippoorwill being so very naughty today? But oh my goodness! Whatever's making that dreadful noise? Surely it can't be Whippoorwill? Not even the naughtiest parrot in the world could make such a flapping din?"

Alice had indeed heard a very flapping din, accompanied by a huge blast of wind which caused the rain to blow hither and thither. Alice was in danger of losing Whippoorwill's stray feather in this hithering and thithering, so she quickly stuffed it back into her pinafore pocket. Something must have passed between the Earth and the Sun just then, because a thick shadow was drifting over Albert Square. Alice looked upwards; a gigantic, steam-driven iron bird was hovering above the world, blotting out the Sun and making terrible noises and gusts with its expansive wings (which were not like ordinary wings, because they didn't flap up and down, rather they flapped round and round and round in a blurred circle of metallic feathers). Alice was sure she could see a large cannon fixed on the front of the bird, and perched on its back—why, it was Mrs Minus and Inspector Jack Russell!

Jack Russell shouted down to Alice, "Give yourself up! Give yourself up!"

Alice would have none of it; she would rather give herself down! She started to run, only to feel a pair of powerful hands clasp around her waist! Alice could not move at all, no matter how hard she struggled! "Get your horrible police-fingers off me!" she shrieked.

"Alice, it's only *you*," croaked a voice behind her.

"Get off me, myself!" Alice shouted to herself.

"Alice, it's me!" replied the voice, releasing the grip. "In other words, it's you! Twin Twisters, remember?"

"Celia!" cried Alice, turning around to recognise her auto-mated counterpart. "I've been searching for you everywhere!"

"I have also been searching for *you* everywhere. Maybe that's why we couldn't find each other until now; everywhere is a ter-ribly large place, don't you agree?"

"I really don't care, Celia!" replied Alice. "Can you please tell me what that hideous iron bird is doing up there?"

"That is a whirlybird," answered Celia, "an automated police-raven. Surely you've heard of the phrase 'The whirlybird catches the wurm'?"

"Well, I've almost heard of the phrase, but please, tell me that isn't a cannon at the front of the whirlybird."

"It *is* a cannon, and we must remove ourselves from this square. Alice, you must look up yourself."

Alice did try her best to *look up* herself, folding her body into a mingle of knots, but all to no avail! And the whirlybird was spiralling ever downwards to the Albert Square, darkening the shadow of itself.

"But wherever shall we remove ourselves to?" cried Alice to Celia.

"We shall remove ourselves to the Central Library of Manchester."

"To find my history, Celia?"

"To look up yourself, Alice. Exactly so! Hold my hand . . ."

∞O

So Alice took hold of Celia's hand, only to be whisked (at a terribly automated speed!) towards the immense, circular Central Library of Manchester! It seemed to Alice that she arrived at the library almost before she set off from the Square. The police-raven did try to keep up with the whizzing young girls, but all it could do was to get itself into a right flap! In fact it was really getting the wind up itself! Alice and Celia laughed to see the fearful mechanical bird struggling in vain with the wind and the rain, and to see Mrs Minus and Inspector Jack Russell struggling to keep hold of their seats! Oh what a joyous sight! Alice and Celia then ducked into the library. (That is to say, a mutated creature—made up of half a man and half an aquatic bird with short legs, large webbed feet, and a broad blunt bill—was waddling through the door at the same time, and Alice and Celia managed to *duck* into the library, under the creature's rather over-large bill!)

SILENCE PLEASE! commanded a sign above the library desk, so

Celia could only whisper hoarsely to Alice, "Don't worry, the whirlybird is too big to get through the door."

"But won't Mrs Minus and Inspector Jack Russell simply bring the whirlybird to the ground?" Alice asked. "And then, won't they simply climb off? And then, won't they simply come to find us on foot?"

"They may simply try to do these things," replied Celia, "but they will find the library to be not at all a *simple* place. They will never find us here amongst the thousands of books, because, this is not only a library, it's also a labyrinth."

"Oh I see," said Alice, "this library is really a *librarinth*?"

"Alice!" cried Celia. "I do believe you are getting used to the language of the future!"

"But I don't want to get used to the future," said Alice. "I want to go back to the past."

"Actually, I quite like it here in the future," Celia proclaimed.

"Celia! Don't you dare say that!"

"But I do."

"Listen to me, Celia. We are both going back to the past, together! Now, please direct me to my history."

"We must ask the librarian about its whereabouts."

The librarian at the desk was a large and stoutly squatted half-frog of a woman, complete with a tweed bonnet on her slimy head and a pair of pince-nez on her slimy nose. Her long, slimy tongue was flicking over the dates on the duckman's books: "These are late, these books!" the frogwoman croaked. "These are late! These books are late back!" She then presented the duckman with a very broad and blunt bill for one hundred and fifty-seven pounds! The duckman started to quack in dismay; he started to argue with the frogwoman. Alice and Celia were still waiting in the queue two minutes later, and getting very impatient as they listened to the quacking and croaking.

Another two minutes later the frog and the duck were still arguing.

"Oh! This is ridiculous!" cried Alice in frustration. "We might as well be queuing by a duck pond!"

"But what else can we do, Alice?" replied Celia. "After all, we *are* English "

"Well I'm tired of being English!" And with that Alice butted in at the counter to ask where in the library she could find—

"Do you mind, young lady?" croaked the frogwoman. "This gentleduck is before you."

"That's right, no butting in, young lady!" quacked the duckman.

Alice glared at the librarian. "Do you realise, Mrs Frog, that I have been a resident in this city for one hundred and thirty-eight years? Surely I'm entitled to a bit of help?"

"Alice, please . . ." hissed Celia.

"Celia! Will you *please* stop bothering me!" cried Alice. "Now, where was I . . . ?"

"But Alice," Celia whispered, "the police are here . . ."

Alice spun around! There indeed were Mrs Minus and Inspector Jack Russell, rushing through the library doors!

"Alice, quickly!" called out Celia, "grab my hand! We must find your book ourselves!"

One grab of an automated hand later, Alice was travelling at speed up some stairs and then along some winding corridors. It was such a spiralling warren of dark and circular tunnels inside the library, that the twistering pair of girls very quickly managed to lose the police, and the sounds of their pursuers dwindled away. However, it was easier to lose something in the librarinth than to find anything. Each of the tunnels wound around a deep shelving of books. Each book bled into a circle of stories, and each story unwound into a maze of words. Alice and Celia went careening around the circulating corridors, looking at spines as they went, looking for the correct book.

One of the books they spotted was called *Waiting for Zo-Zo,* another was called *Butcher in the Pie,* another *The Whirl Uncording to Carp.* Here are some more books they saw in their search: *Hatch 22, The Gnome of the Hose, Stoat Fishing in Amirrorca, From Cher to Infirmity, How to Forsake Friends and Unfluence People, The Upping Street Tears, Useless-ease, Fooligans Wake, Merde sur la Nile* (in French), *The Waistlined, Das Typical, The Zen of Auto-Horse Maintenance, Withering Kites, Wildhood's End, 2001—A Bass Odyssey, The Bargain Hoods of Hay, Midget's Children, Crêpe Expectations, The Holy Bubble* (including the Mould Infestment and the Nude Jestament), *Five Go Off to Damp, Not a Penny More, Not a Penny Less.*

"Celia, these book titles make *no sense at all!*" complained Alice. "Especially that last one!"

"Well you did call this place a librarinth, Alice," replied Celia, slowing down to a standstill in yet another dusty room of books.

"Not only no sense," stated Alice, letting go of her friend's hand, "but also no kind of order at all!"

"You think not, Alice?"

"Neither alphabetical order by title; nor alphabetical order by author."

"Or even subject, Alice."

"Exactly, Celia: no order at all! What is the use of such a random library? How can anybody find the book they want?"

"I suspect there is an order to the librarinth, Alice, otherwise how could the *librarinthians* locate the books at all?"

"But if the order isn't by title or author or subject, what can it be?"

"Maybe it's a secret order, Alice, known only to the librarinthians? Maybe the order's waiting for us to find it."

"But how can we do that?"

"We examine, Alice. We use logic. We take a row of books, and then we analyse them for coincidences."

"Very well then," said Alice, gruffly, taking down three books from the nearest shelf. "Here are three books. Analyse these, if you can!"

"I will most certainly try . . ."

The three adjacent books that Alice selected for Celia were called *The Twenty-Seven of Spades, Descriptions of Cheese Funnels* and *Elsewhere in the Noonyvurt.* Celia studied these three books for exactly two seconds and then announced, proudly, "Of course! How could I be so stupid!"

(The reader may like to join in the game before reading on, and pause to consider the connecting principle of the three books.)

"You mean you've found out how the librarinth is arranged?" asked Alice.

"It's so obvious!"

"Well, it's not at all obvious to me!" said Alice, rather vexed.

(Has the reader worked it out yet?)

"But surely you can see it, Alice?"

"No, I can't, Celia. Please tell me."

(Has the reader still not analysed it?)

"Very well," began Celia. "The books in this library are arranged according to the last three letters in their titles. Consider the first book, *The Twenty-Seven of Spades:* it ends in *d . . . e . . . s.* Consider the second book, *Descriptions of Cheese Funnels:* it starts with *D . . . e . . . s;* and then it ends with *e . . . l . . . s.* Consider the third book, *Elsewhere in the Noonyvurt:* it begins with *E . . . l . . . s.* Is that not conclusive proof, Alice, of my terbo-charged intelligence?"

"It would be," replied Alice, "except that the next book along the shelf, according to you, must begin with the letters *U . . . r . . . t.* And that can't be possible!"

Celia reached up for the next book on the shelf, pulled it down and wordlessly showed it to Alice.

The book was called, not so wordlessly, *Urtext Shurt.*

"Well, I know what a Shurt is," said Alice; "it's a book by a writer of Wrongs called Mister Zenith O'Clock: but what is an Urtext?"

"Well, urtext is a German word, meaning the earliest form of a text. In other words, *Urtext Shurt* is an earlier version of the book called *Shurt.* Your Mister O'Clock must have deposited his first drafts in the library."

"Your mind is very active at the moment, Celia."

"I don't have a mind, I have a mound. And my computer-

mites *are* rather tingling with all the exercise. Let's try to find
the book of your life, Alice. What do you know about it?"

"I know that the book of my life is called *Reality and Realicey*.
That means it must come after a book ending in *r . . . e . . . a,*
and before a book beginning in *C . . . e . . . y.* Now what could
they possibly be called? Wait a minute!" And Alice did a little
jump, quite startling herself. "I have the answer! Whippoorwill's last riddle was this: Who is it that lives between An
Octopus's Area and Ceylon's Favourite Stethoscope? Why, that
must be *Reality and Realicey,* mustn't it?"

"Well done, Alice!"

"Now, all we have to do is find a book called *An Octopus's Area*
and a book called *Ceylon's Favourite Stethoscope,* and the book in
between them will be called *Reality and Realicey*—the story of
my life!"

"This is a librarinth, remember, Alice? A book called *Reality
and Realicey* could also be perched between two books called *A
Squid's Area* and *Ceylon's Favourite Teacup,* or *Ceylon's Favourite
Anything!* In the librarinth there is an infinitude of letters and
spaces. All words, however misspelt, exist within these walls.
The possibilities are endless."

"But Celia, I don't want the possibilities to be endless, I want
them to end exactly upon the place where the book called
Reality and Realicey lies."

"Stay calm, my dearest Alice," whispered Celia then, "and
take my hand; I think we might have found some help . . ."

The help they found was Whippoorwill the parrot, of course, whom Celia had spotted flying along a corridor. A moment later Alice was flying *herself*, along with her automated sister, along the twisting tunnels of the librarinth, after Whippoorwill. Around and around and around the whirl of books they went, chasing the parrot. Until, eventually, he flew upwards into the roof of the building, and there he vanished through an open skylight!

"We've lost him!" squealed Alice, catching her breath.

"He must have been leading us somewhere," replied Celia. "After all, he knew all about the area of an octopus and the favourite stethoscope of Ceylon."

Alice pulled down the nearest book: it was called *Crocus and Chairless*. "Celia, this book is nowhere near to my *Reality and Realicey!*"

"Examine the next book along," urged Celia.

The next book along was *Essex Excess;* the one after that was called *Essential Modes of Rocking Chair Leathers;* the next after that, *Ersatz Marbles*. Alice was by this time pulling out book after book after book, and casting them all to the ground! *Lessons in Wonderment, Entries to Bliss, Issues of Mischief Paper, Perhaps the Curtains Are Crimson, Son of the Son of Monster Magnet, Nettles and Binoculars (a User's Primer), Mercurial Teeth and How to Shave Them, Hemlines Through the Ages, Gesticulating Ogre, Great Ways to Cook Bacon, Considering Breakfast, Asterisk and the History of Disco, Scooping for Boys, Oysters in Trousers, Ersatz Trousers, Ersatz Pinafores, Rescuing Books from Libraries (a How-to Guide), Ideals in Kippers, Erstwhile Manchester . . .*

Book after book after book . . . Alice pulling a storm of
leaves off the shelves . . .

*Termite Control (Advanced), Cedar Control (Moronic), Nicotine
Knitwear and Smoking Trumpet Control (Advanced Moronic), Nice
and Easy Does It (Advanced Moronic and Clock-Rush), Usherettes of
Tomorrow.*

"The book of my life is nowhere to be seen!" cried Alice,
pulling out even more books, as the piles of books on the floor
grew and grew. *Rowing to Bleak House, Use of Loose Moose in a
Kitchen, Henry the Eighth and His Sixteen Wives* . . .

"Keep looking, my Alice," replied Celia, calmly.
"Whippoorwill surely has a plan . . ."

More books pulled off: *Vest Sores, Rescuing Books from Libraries
(Volume Seven), Venus Guitars, Ars Gratia Artis, Tissue Ellipsis,
Sisterly Forever* . . .

"Celia, I do believe we're getting closer!" cried Alice, crush-
ing books underfoot to reach *Vertical Piano Playing,* and then
Ingots of Gold, and then *Olden Times, Messages from Jupiter,
Terminal Guano.* "Yes! Here it is!" screamed Alice, pulling out
the next book along: *An Octopus's Area.* But when Alice pulled
the next book down from the shelf, imagine her disappoint-
ment to find that it was called *Ceylon's Favourite Stethoscope!* "But
this is all wrong!" stamped Alice. "This book should be called
Reality and Realicey!"

"It should be," Celia murmured, "but it isn't. Look, Alice,
there's a gap where your book should have been . . ."

"But what does that mean, Celia?"

"It means, Alice, that somebody has borrowed your history."

"How dare they!" cried Alice. "I shall never be able to look up myself now!"

OCO

Alice was crying so much that Celia had to clamp her porcelain fingers over her twin twister's mouth. "Alice, will you keep quiet!" she whispered. "We are in a *library,* remember. Shush! You'll disturb the other readers . . ."

(The reader will have only just noticed the other readers, for the simple fact that I forgot to mention them previously. Oh dear, I am getting forgetful in my old age. Never mind, let me show you the several mixed-up this-and-that creatures that were studying their chosen books at various tables. They were all looking up at Alice with glaring eyes: why, some of them were even pointedly pointing towards the SILENCE PLEASE! sign.)

"I don't care about the other readers!" Alice sobbed. "Oh Celia! Just when we were so close to finding it, as well!"

"I know! It is a bother, isn't it?" Celia croaked, kindly. "But look, there's a funny little fishman over at that table—a plaice-man, I believe—and he's fast asleep! Now you wouldn't want to waken him, would you? That would be rude."

Alice mopped up some of her tears with her pinafore, and then sauntered over to the fishman. Celia followed, wondering what Alice was hoping to achieve by gently tapping like that on the fishman's shoulder? (Now then, the question of the exact position of a fish's shoulders; this is the riddle that has puzzled ichthyologists—the Examiners of Fish—down the ages, and I shan't go into it here.) Suffice it to say that Alice did tap on the fishman's shoulders, achieving no response at all. "Celia . . ." Alice breathed, "I do believe this plaiceman is dead."

"What makes you say that, Alice," asked Celia.

"Firstly, I can't waken him; secondly, his left fin is sprouting from his forehead; thirdly, his gills are where his eyes should be; and fourthly, his tail is flopping out of his mouth!"

"Alice, you have become *automated* to the subject of death!" said Celia.

"It's time for us both to grow up," Alice responded. "This poor plaiceman has been Jigsaw Murdered, and that is a crime. And look! He's got a jigsaw piece clutched in his right fin. It's one of my missing ones: a fish's fin belonging in the aquarium of my London Zoo puzzle. And look! He's slumped over a book called *Reality and Realicey!* Oh Celia, maybe I've finally found my place in history?"

IX

THE HUNTING

OF THE QUARK

THE other readers were making a racket-ing protest by now (despite the SILENCE PLEASE! signs) at Alice's shouts of jubilation. Alice paid them no mind at all; instead she quickly added the fishy jigsaw piece to the other seven in her pinafore pocket, and gently slid the history book from under the fishman's glistening (and rather smelly) body. The book called *Reality and Realicey* was so large and thick and fish-stained that Alice had a rare time trying to get it open at the first page; but eventually she managed to reach the first sen-tence of the book, and this is what she read:

> The Reality set is a subset of the Existence set,
> which also contains the Unreality set and the
> Nureality set. The three subsets of Existence
> correspond exactly to the three subsets of
> Alistence, namely: the Real Alice, the
> Imagined Alice and the Automated Alice.

"Celia?" Alice called out, upon reaching the end of the pas-sage, "could you please explain these words to me?" But Celia was suddenly nowhere to be seen! "Celia, where have you vanished to this time? Oh, but I haven't got time to be chas-ing that doll just now—and there simply isn't enough time in the whole of history to read this entire book—so I think I'll skip through all the pages until I reach the last one; surely *there* I'll find my answer?" Of course Alice didn't quite skip through the pages, because they were so heavy; it was more like a trudge through sludge, but eventually she managed to reach the last lines of the book, and this is what she read there:

> . . . by which time the Real and the Imagined Alices were indistinguishable in Lewis Carroll's mind. This confusion caused him to project the combined Alices into the future. Only by sending Alice on one final epic journey in search of her past, back into childhood's dream, so to speak, could he hope to cleanse his own imagination in the dying moments of a mental ellipsis . . .

"Oh, poppycock!" exclaimed Alice. "This is no help at all! Why, the author has ended this giant of a book with an ellipsis! Surely there cannot be more to be said on the subject! Who wrote this rubbish?" (Alice was becoming really rather *modern* by this time.) She heaved the book shut in order to look at the front cover more closely.

Reality and Realicey, it said, by Professor Gladys Chrowdingler.

"Professor Chrowdingler wrote this!" Alice shrieked. "Why, she's one of the things I'm searching for!" Alice once again wrestled with the book, until she forced it to turn to the inside back cover. There she found a photograph of an aged pipe-sucking crow-woman in a bowler hat, and below the picture, a brief biography of the author:

Gladys Chrowdingler was born in 1910. Her previous best-selling tomes include *Oz and Ozzification, Pooh and Poohtrefaction* and *Peter Pandemonia*. She is currently Professor of Chrownotransductionology at the Uniworseity of Manchester. She lives with a cat called Quark, who sometimes helps with experiments.

"Now then," Alice thought, "I'm sure that I passed the Uni*ver*sity of Manchester on my police-auto journey into the city: perhaps the Uni*worse*ity of Manchester could be somewhere near to that? Surely I must go there to find this Professor called Chrowdingler. But however shall I manage it in time?"

Just then Celia came thumping down a book-lined corridor. "Alice, quickly!" the Automated Alice croaked out, "we must make our escape: the police are here!" At which all the other readers vanished like bookworms into the deeply tangled word-tunnels.

"Where are they?" gasped Alice, looking around in a panic.

"Suddenly everywhere!" answered Celia.

Indeed the police *were* suddenly everywhere! They were creeping out of every alleyway, every tunnel, every single maze-path of the librarinth. In no time at all, Alice and Celia were completely surrounded by a champing circle of dog officers. Mrs Minus and Inspector Jack Russell emerged from the ragged circumference. Mrs Minus was snakely fingering the corpse of the aquatic reader. "Girl Alice," the subtracter snake hissed, "you are under arrest for Hindering the Police in Their

Enquiries. You are further under arrest for the Jigsaw Murder of this poor innocent fishman."

"Oh, what shall we do now, Celia?" pleaded Alice.

"Open up the cupboard in my right-hand thigh," whispered Celia.

"I didn't know you had a cupboard in your right-hand thigh!"

"Pablo Ogden made many rearrangements to my body. Take a little look."

So Alice did take a little look. Upon Celia's right-hand thigh was a small cupboard door, labelled TO BE OPENED IN AN EMERGENCY ONLY.

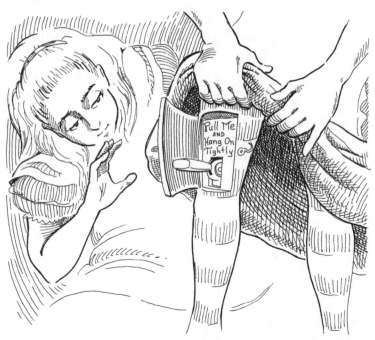

"I don't know what's in there," Celia croaked, "but won't you please open it up, Alice? The police are closing in!"

The police *were* closing in!

So Alice opened up the cupboard in Celia's thigh. There she found a shiny brass lever, and above it the message PULL ME AND HANG ON TIGHTLY! Alice pulled the lever . . .

Four-and-a-fearsome minutes later, Alice and Celia were speeding down the Oxford Road in search of the Uniworseity of Manchester. And there was Whippoorwill the parrot, fluttering along just ahead of them, always just so tantalisingly out of reach. Police sirens were singing a plaintive song through the rain, but Celia was running at such a terbo-charged speed that the twinly-twisted pair very soon escaped from their pursuers.

Six-and-a-slickety minutes later, Alice and Celia arrived at the imposing stone-built bulk of the University of Manchester. Once inside the campus, they managed (of course!) to lose Whippoorwill, but also managed to *find* a series of hand-painted signs that led them towards a small hole in the ground, marked with a downwards pointing arrow: THE UNIWORSEITY THIS WAY.

Down the hole Alice and her twin twister went.

(Dearest readers, in my old age I seem to have mislaid the passage that tells of what happened when Alice pulled the lever in Celia's right-hand thigh. I must now deliver that story to you; or else the reader will surely bang shut this final Book of Alice in frustration.)

Pablo Ogden had kitted-out the Automated Alice with two thigh-cupboards, the left and the right. The left-leg cupboard was marked with the words TO BE OPENED IN AN *EXTREME* EMERGENCY ONLY. The right-leg cupboard was to be opened in a lesser-than-extreme emergency, and this was the door that Alice had opened, revealing the shiny brass lever, which Alice pulled . . .

Celia's legs then started to grow up like two tree trunks, towards the ceiling of the librarinth! Alice clung onto these telescoping legs, as Celia towered towards the skylight, through which Whippoorwill the parrot had previously flown. Ever so high! Alice looked down (always a mistake) and felt quite giddy from the upwards-rushing journey.

The policedogmen were left far down below, where they could only pant and growl in frustration. Alice waved goodbye to them, with a smile. Once on the roof of the library, Celia collapsed her extended legs back into a neat porcelain pair, and then *re*extended them over the side of the building so that Alice and herself could descend to the road below. Once safely on the ground, Celia folded up her legs to their usual size, and from there the two adventuring girls raced along the Oxford Road towards the University and its underfolded passages . . .

(I do hope I've remembered that little escapade correctly.)

The Uni*worse*ity; a darkling underworld of glimmers and shimmers, a myriad of shadows pointing Alice and Celia towards a laboratory called THE DEPARTMENT OF CHROWNO-TRANSDUCTIONOLOGY. Alice knocked on the door and received no answer except for a far-off *cawing;* she pushed open the door and walked, quite brazenly, into the laboratory.

These are some of the things that Alice and Celia found in there: a whole concoction of scientific apparatus wriggling and steaming and fuming in every single corner of the laboratory; a giant heap of computermites noisily chomping their way through a series of terrifically difficult questions; waves of liquid mystery bubbling along a knotwork of glass pipes, until they all inserted themselves into a large wooden box that rested on the floor; some black lettering on the box's side that said DANGEROUS EXPERIMENT!; a dirty black dishcloth of an old crow that was perching on the box's lid (and wearing a bowler hat, mind!), cawing away to itself, whilst at the same time smoking a Meerschaum pipe. "Quark, quark!" rasped the crow, through clouding wreaths of tobacco mist.

But the very worst thing that Alice found in the laboratory was the smell! Oh dear, the smell! It was the stench that can sometimes be emitted from the *wrong end of a ghastly meat pie,* in the high season.

The crow was tap-tap-tapping on the wooden box's lid with the pipe in her nicotined beak. "It's very smelly in here!" Alice commented to the crow, not expecting any answer, and receiving none, except for a further tippety-tapping. "And I was *so* hoping to find Professor Gladys Chrowdingler!" Alice added.

At which point the crow flopped off the box with a piercing cry, "Quark!" And by the time the bird had landed at Alice's feet, it had turned into a fully grown crow-woman: an ancient, creased-up crone of a human woman, complete with a crow's beak-and-wing accessories (and a bowler-hatted accompaniment).

"I am Professor Gladys Chrowdingler!" the crow-woman quarked mightily, taking the steaming pipe out of her mouth for a moment (and tipping her bowler hat to the two Alices). "The horrible smell  comes from my chemical and physical experiments, I'm afraid. Oh, but I'm so glad that you two girls have safely arrived in my lab; I've been waiting ages for you! Ages! Now then, which of you is the *Reality* Alice?"

The crow-woman flapped at Alice and Celia with her wings of soot.

Alice had noticed that something was trapped inside the wooden box. It was banging against the insides, demanding, in a muffled voice, to be let out. Alice decided to ignore the thing in the box for the moment. "Why, *I'm* the real Alice, of course," she told the Professor.

"Are you sure?" asked the crow-woman, speaking around the fuming pipe she had replaced in her beak. "You both look almost identical."

"*She* is the real Alice," Celia stated plainly, and pointed. "I'm only the Automated version; my name is Celia."

"Yes, that's right," said Alice, equally plainly (although, to be honest, the real-life Alice was becoming a little confused), "and we have come here from the past to ask you the way back home."

"Quark, quark!" quarked the crow-woman, impatiently. "Alice, have you read my book in the library, pray?"

"Yes, I have, and that's exactly how I managed to find you."

"Excellent! The plan is unfolding!"

"That is . . . to be honest . . ." hesitated Alice, "I've only read the beginning and the end of your book."

"That will suffice for now. Your final story will continue; the timely plan is being mapped-out."

"What do you mean," queried Alice, "by my *final* story? And what is this plan that you keep mentioning?"

"You know that Lewis Carroll invented you, Alice, in his books called *Wonderland* and *Looking-Glass*?" asked Chrowdingler.

"Well, yes . . . I mean, only *partly* so."

"Splendid answer! You are more than halfway there!"

"Halfway where?" asked Alice.

"Halfway to not being merely an *Alias Alice,* of course. Don't you see it?"

"I'm *trying* to see it. But really, Professor Chrowdingler, all I want to do is to get back to the past."

"Of course you do! That is your nature, Alice: that is what Lewis Carroll instilled in your soul."

"But I'm not just Lewis Carroll's invention; I'm real as well!"

"Alice, you are both real and imagined, and also automated. Your real persona is called Alice Liddell; your unreal persona is called Alice in Wonderland; your nureal persona is called Celia Hobart."

"I didn't know Celia had a second name," said Alice.

"Neither did I!" croaked Celia (rather proudly) before asking, "What does nureal mean, Professor?"

"Nureality is a recent discovery of mine," answered the
Professor. "A place where things can live halfway between reality and unreality. I invented the place because of the increas-
ing population of the terbots, you see? Creatures like yourself,
Automated Alice, are you real or unreal? Is there such a thing
as an artificial intelligence? Basically, the question . . . can a
mechanical being be deemed to live?"

"Well . . . I feel that I'm alive," responded Celia.

"Exactly so! You *feel* your aliveness, Automated Alice, therefore you are alive! You are at home with yourself! This is why I
discovered the new state of nureality. Reality Alice, on the other
wing . . ." (and here the old Professor waved a blackly dismissive
unfolding of feathers at Alice) "is neither here nor there. This
little girl isn't sure if she's real, or else just a finishing story and
plan inside Mister Lewis Carroll's head. He wrote one final
book, you see, in his old age: a book called *Automated Alice*. In
this lingering tome he brought Reality Alice to the future of
now; he brought her into 1998! And in this final book, the
author deemed it necessary that Alice should meet up with a
Professor called Chrowdingler! Quark! Oh, I'm so excited!"

Alice decided things were getting out of hand. "Professor
Chrowdingler," she interrupted, "would you please tell me
how to get home to the past, in time to complete my two
o'clock writing lesson?"

"Quark! Am I right to assume, Alice, that you ate some
radishes this morning?"

"I did actually," replied Alice, "but it was only a jammy spoonful."

"No matter at all, Alice! That is how you have come to visit the future: you have partaken of the Radishes of Time! They had chrownons within them."

"Whatever do you mean? What are chrownons?"

"Quark, quark!" answered Professor Chrowdingler.

Alice suddenly remembered something she had read on the inside back cover of *Reality and Realicey*. "Professor Chrowdingler," she asked, "are you hunting for your cat, by any chance?"

"You bet I am! Now where *is* that pesky feline? Quark!" Chrowdingler began hunting all around as she said this; all around the twisting pipes of her scientifical equipment; all around the stenching fog of gases emitted from spitting pipes; even all around the backside of the wooden box. "Here, kitty kitty!" cawed the Professor, holding aloft a piece of raw pork. "It's dinner time, my little Quark!"

Alice thought it very unusual that a crow should have a cat as a pet, but she didn't mention it. Instead, she asked, "Why is your cat called Quark?"

"Well . . ." began the Professor, "a quark is a set of hypothetical elementary particles, postulated to be the fundamental and invisible units of all carryons and chrownons. Do you understand, Alice? It's quite simple: every single thing that exists is made out of tiny particles; and a quark is the invisible unit inside of every *carryon* particle, and also inside of every *chrownon*. The strangest thing about quarks is that we scientists know that they *do* exist, but we don't know *where* they exist!"

"That sounds rather too much like a certain parrot I know," said Alice.

"Quark, quark!" quarked Chrowdingler, "come home to me, my kitten!" But the pet of a cat was nowhere to be seen. "This is why I called my cat *Quark*," said the Professor to Alice, "because he was always so very prone to vanishing: and nothing can vanish quicker than a fundamental particle! I was doing an experiment, you see: one which tried to register the impact of the carryon particles on the innocent people of Manchester. The experiment entailed the encapturing of my pet cat in this particular box of tricks . . ." Professor Chrowdingler was tapping with her pipe upon the wooden box's lid; from within the box's interior came a further dismal call for help.

"So you placed your pet cat inside this box . . ." croaked Celia, "and then what did you do?"

"I funnelled a cloud of carryon particles into the box."

"And what is a carryon, when it's at home?" asked Alice.

"A carryon is the particle that allows the various species to mate with each other. This is why we are all currently suffering from the Newmonia."

"So you're a carryon crow?" pondered Alice.

"Exactly so! I uncovered and named that particle after myself."

"And this is where the disease called the Newmonia came from?"

"That's right; the Civil Serpents introduced the carryon particle into the nation's wavey length: they were hoping to make the populace succumb to quietude, I guess. The original idea was to turn everybody into gentle, law-abiding mice-people:

this inexact science is known as Djinnetic Engineering, on account of it being not unlike letting a rabid genie out of a bottle. The serpents' silly experiment went dreadfully wrong of course, and the rampant carryon particle transformed the people into a mishmash of mutated creatures. My crowly shape is just one of the various outcomes. So it was that I devised this boxly experiment, containing both a domestic cat and a fog of the dreaded carryon particles."

"But your experimental cat must have mewled and spat at being forced inside the box of carryons?" claimed Celia.

"Oh, how my little Quark mewled and spat! But really, I was only trying to prove the usage of carryon particles in the dissipation of the Newmonia disease. But my dear Quark was viciously attacked by the carryons!"

"What happened then?" asked Alice.

"Quark was mixed up with a chameleon's nature."

Just then, Alice noticed a translucent *something* moving through the scientifical equipment on one of Chrowdingler's workbenches. It looked very much like the nebulous smile of a feline beauty, long since admitted to the disappearing realms of catouflage. A soft and plaintive "Meowwwlll!" came out of nowhere as something unseen and furry knocked over a test tube. "Quark, Quark!" screeched Chrowdingler upon the evidence of her phantom cat's misdemeanour. The Professor made a feathery-fluttering move to trap the ghostly cat, ending up with only a few wisps of figmental fur in her pointed beak.

"Quark is an invisible cat!" cried Alice, recalling a certain incident in one of her previous adventures. (Although, never

in the life of her, would she have suspected that one day in the future she would discover a scientific reason for the old Cheshire Cat's disappearance!)

"Quite so!" cawed the crow. "Quark has become a chamelecat."

"So it's the Civil Serpents who are to blame for the Newmonia disease?" asked Alice, returning (finally) to the subject.

"That's correct," replied Chrowdingler. "The Civil Serpents tried their very best to cover up the carryon mistake, claiming the pandemonious Newmonia disease to be no more than a natural aberration of nature. There are only twelve beings in the whole world that know of the serpents' real misdeed."

Twelve! Alice, suddenly enlightened, asked, "Would these twelve beings include a computermite and a ramshackle badgerman and a sleepy snake? And would they also include a chicken-powered terbot musician and a zebraman and a long-distance snailman? Also, a spiderboy and a catwoman and a bookish plaiceman?"

"They would indeed!" answered Chrowdingler. "The Civil Serpents are determined to kill off all of the knowledgeable twelve, in order to hide their misuse of the carryon particles, and their ghastly crimes against humanity. Quark! The serpents are determined to kill off every single carrier of the carryon clue; this includes myself of course. Very soon the Snakes of Law will rearrange my body into a deathly puzzle." With this utterance Chrowdingler reached into her wing's darkness to produce a little piece of jagged wood: "This arrived in the post this very morning . . ."

It was the jigsawed fragment from the aviary in the London Zoo puzzle, showing a crow's black feather. Alice took it quite *pleasingly*. "Oh, thank you, Professor, for delivering this jigsaw piece to me!" she cried. "I now have nine of my twelve missing pieces!"

"To be given such a jigsaw piece," warned the Professor, "implies that the Civil Serpents will be wanting to kill you off for your dangerous knowledge. These are the jigsaw pieces of Cain!"

"But all along I thought the Civil Serpents," queried Celia, "had been urging the police to find the Jigsaw Murderer? Isn't this why they arrested Captain Ramshackle, and also Alice's poor, innocent, real self?"

"The police are ignorant of the real murderer, and the real crime. The serpents are merely looking for escape-goats."

Alice dearly wanted to ask what an escape-goat was, but at that very moment, from the insides of the wooden box, came once more a shrill voice that pleaded, "Please let me out of this box!"

"I'm not letting you out of the box so early!" screeked the crow-woman in reply. "The experiment is not yet over!" Simultaneously to this screeking, there was also a terrible pounding on the stairs that led down to the Uniworseity of Manchester. "This is the Civil Serpents!" pounded the pounding. "Alice Liddell and Professor Chrowdingler! You are both under arrest for the Jigsaw Murders!"

The pipe fell out of Chrowdingler's mouth! "Quickly, Alice!" she urged. "This is what you have to do next: you must find the remaining *three* of your missing jigsaw pieces. You must then take all twelve of the pieces to your Great Aunt's house in Didsbury village. Promise me that you *will* carry all twelve of the pieces to your puzzle back to the past, because only *then* will we futurites be saved from the serpents' wrath!"

"We promise, Professor Chrowdingler," croaked Celia.

"But my tenth jigsaw piece is with the Civil Serpents!" added the real Alice. "They are keeping it for evidence at the Town Hall."

"So to the Town Hall must you journey!" screeked the crow-woman in a flurry of wing-beats. "But now you must hide inside the experiment-box."

"I'm not getting in *there!*" announced Alice in a huff. But the pounding of the serpents on the stairs caused Celia to add (in a second huff!), "But Alice! it's our only chance to escape!" Celia opened up the box's lid and climbed inside.

"But Professor," hesitated Alice, "you haven't yet told us about the chrownon particles."

"I haven't the time for that," replied Chrowdingler.

And so Alice (rather nervously) followed Celia into the box.

SNAKES

AND

LEADERS

IT was very dark inside the box, and very cramped, so much so that Alice couldn't see her own nose in front of her face! But her unseen nose *could* smell a waft of sickly talcum powder. "Captain Ramshackle!" cried Alice to the darkness, upon smelling that dusty aroma, "it was *you* in here, trying to find a way out!"

"Indeed it is my very own self, trying to escape," answered the boxed-up badgerman from the darkness.

"But what are you doing inside here?" questioned Alice.

"I was hoping to follow the example of Quark the cat," came the miserable, invisible reply.

"In order to make yourself invisible to the Civil Serpents . . . ?"

"Precisely so!" admitted Ramshackle. "I was hoping that Professor Chrowdingler could turn me into a badgermeleon! Am I correct to suspect that the experiment has failed?"

"I suspect, Captain Ramshackle," said Alice, "that you are no more invisible than I am! And that is not very invisible at all! Even though it's completely dark in this dangerous box!"

"What's happening outside the box?" whispered Ramshackle, fearfully.

"The Civil Serpents have come to find us," whispered Celia, hoarsely.

"Who are you?!" cried Ramshackle. "Are there two Alices in the box?"

"This is my automated sister, Captain," introduced Alice. "She's called Celia."

"Alice has been split in two?!"

"Well yes," answered Alice, "I suppose I have."

"How superbly random that must be!" exclaimed the bad-german, finding a little of his old bravado. "Should we look outside just yet, do you think?"

"No, we should not!" cried Alice, as something heavy started hammering! on the roof of the box. "Is there a way to lock this box from the inside?"

"There is indeed . . ." responded Ramshackle, reaching upwards to turn a small latch on the box's ceiling.

The noise from outside seemed to recede. Alice felt safe enough to ask some questions. "What do you know about the Radishes of Time, Captain Ramshackle?" was her first enquiry.

"Professor Chrowdingler told me nearly everything that she knew. The Radishes of Time are where the chrownon particles live and breed."

"And what is a chrownon?" asked Alice with her second question.

"A chrownon is another particle that Chrowdingler has uncovered: it is the elementary unit of time itself! My dear Alice . . . you must have eaten some forwards chrownons in the past; this is why you have travelled to 1998! To get back to 1860, you would have to swallow some backwards chrownons."

"I must swallow a radish, backwards?" protested Alice with her third question.

"That is correct, and you must swallow them at the very place of your leaving, and at the very same time as your leaving."

"In other words, Alice," explained Celia, helpfully, "we must travel to your Great Aunt's house in Didsbury. Once there, we must eat some of the radishes in your Great Uncle's vegetable patch, and we have to do all of this at precisely two o'clock."

"Your automated sister is most wise," said Ramshackle. "This whole process, according to Chrowdingler, is known as *Chrownotransductionology;* in other words: timely travel."

Just then, Alice's nose noticed a pungent whiff of gas over and above the badger's talcum waft. "Have you made a social *faux pas,* Captain?" she discreetly enquired.

"No, I have not made a social fart-pants!" pleaded the badgerman.

"Captain Ramshackle!" cried Alice, "one should not say such things!"

"You said it first!"

"I did not! I said *faux pas!* It's quite different: why, it's *French,* for one thing! Therefore it's much more polite!" Alice was here following her Great Aunt's instructions in etiquette. (Great Uncle Mortimer did eat an *awful* amount of radishes, remember?)

"In the future, Alice . . ." explained Celia, "there are hardly any words at all that cannot be said aloud. Why, you can even say—"

"Well I don't like the future," Alice cut in. "It's beastly, and I want to go home!"

"Sisters, sisters! This is not the smell of my netherness," said Ramshackle; "this is the smell of carryon gas, seeping into the box."

Alice screamed: "I don't want to be changed! I don't want to catch Newmonia! I want to be just me!" She nudged open the latch and began to push against the lid.

Oh dear! The box wouldn't open!

Alice pushed and pushed, but still the lid wouldn't open. It wouldn't budge, not an inch! "The Civil Serpents have locked us in!" she cried, as the rotten smell of carryons stenched up her nostrils. "Celia, quickly! We must pull your right-hand thigh-cupboard lever once again: perhaps your telescoping legs will break open the lid . . ."

"I'm afraid I can use each of my thigh-cupboards only once," was Celia's reply to *that* suggestion.

"We must open your left-hand thigh-cupboard then!"

"But that cupboard is to be used only in an extreme emergency."

"This is an *extremely* extreme emergency!"

"I'm not so sure it is, Alice," said Ramshackle. "Maybe if we all three of us pushed together, we could get out?"

So all three of them did push together, and lo and behold! The box wasn't locked at all, the Civil Serpents had merely placed something very heavy on top of it. This heavy something fell to the floor with a dull thud! as the trio opened up the lid in order to peer (surreptitiously!) over the box's rim . . .

The laboratory was quite empty.

Alice (and then Celia in a pair of nervous brackets) ((and then Captain Ramshackle, in a pair of doubly nervous brackets)) climbed out of the experiment-box. They all seemed quite unchanged by their adventure. "I do believe the carryon gas needs much longer than that to work," explained Ramshackle.

"Oh dear!" whispered Celia, as she noticed what exactly they had dislodged from the lid to the floor . . .

It was the corpse of Professor Gladys Chrowdingler! The crow-woman's wings were now flapping lifelessly from either side of her eyes! Her sooty tail was sprouting from her lips! Her eyes were lifelessly peering from each of her knees!

"The Professor has been Jigsaw Murdered!" cried Celia. "The Civil Serpents have reorganized her!"

And the laboratory wasn't quite so empty, because Alice saw a certain translucent whispering of fur rubbing against the Professor's mixed-up body. Alice picked up the translucent whispering, gently, and began to stroke it. (Have you ever tried to stroke an invisible cat? I can assure you it's a very strange task; but if anybody could do it, Alice could, and Alice *did* do it . . .) For some almost unknown reason Alice was the only one of her party who could see anything at all of Quark, the Invisible Cat. The cat purred at being treated so kindly. "You'll have to find your own way in the world now, invisible puss-cat," Alice said, lowering the cat to the floor. Alice then turned to Captain Ramshackle. "What time is it, please?" she enquired of him. Ramshackle rolled up his left shirt-sleeve to reveal a little wrist-clock there. "It's almost exactly one o'clock in the afternoon," he answered.

"I therefore have only sixty minutes in which to find the tenth, spidery jigsaw piece," deduced Alice, catching hold of

Celia's hand, "and then the eleventh parroty piece, and then the mysterious twelfth and final piece. Quickly, Celia . . . activate your automated speeding legs: back to the Town Hall of Manchester we must travel!"

"I'm coming with you," said Captain Ramshackle, trying to climb aboard the doll's already moving body. But Alice pushed him back gently. "This is my task alone, Captain," she informed him. "Don't worry: I shall try my very best to save you from the serpents . . ."

∞○

It took Alice and Celia only a single few minutes to journey the distance from the Uniworseity to the Town Hall. Alice's first problem was exactly how to get inside the Town Hall, without the Civil Serpents knowing she was there. To this end she had instructed Celia to deliver her to the side courtyard of the building, where a small door marked with a sign admitting DELIVERIES ONLY! was guarded by the unravelling eightfoldness of an octopusman. This bouncing individual waved his collection of long legs around in a dance of clinging suckers, squelching out with a soapy voice, "What has this young girl to deliver, I wonder?"

"I'm delivering the new mascot for Mrs Minus's election campaign," invented Alice, pushing Celia forwards. "A vote for Mrs Minus," announced Celia, in her most *political* voice, "is a vote for subtraction!"

"Let me check this delivery," over-emphasised the octopusman: at which he blubbered into a brass mouth-horn fixed to

the Delivery Door's interior passage. A slithering voice answered back to him, and then the octopusman said to Alice, "You may (carefully!) enter . . ."

So it was that Alice and Celia gained a careful entrance to the Town Hall of Manchester. It was very echoey and also very cold inside those hallowed corridors: it was a stonely warren of wonderings through which the pair of them echoed like copies of themselves. The strangest thing of all about the Town Hall was that they met absolutely nobody at all along their way! "I always imagined that a town hall would be a very *busy* building," echoed Alice. "Perhaps they do their business in secret?" echoed Celia. Eventually Alice and Celia passed under a sign reading THE PRUNING DEPARTMENT to enter a large echoing room of emptiness.

"Where should we head for now, Celia?" echoed Alice, pondering upon a signpost that sprouted directions for THE TREASURING DEPARTMENT, THE WHISPERING DEPARTMENT, THE TORTURING DEPARTMENT, THE TAXING DEPARTMENT AND THE SLEAZING DEPARTMENT.

"I suspect that the department we're seeking won't be signposted," echoed Celia. "We know that the Civil Serpents keep their evidence in the cellar of the Town Hall, so maybe it's THE PLUMMETING DEPARTMENT we need to find?"

"But if a department isn't signposted, how can we find it? Oh, if only I had a single clue!"

At which Celia suddenly cried, "Alice! Look at the floor!"

Alice looked at the floor. "My goodness," she echoed, for the marble floor they were standing on was carefully tiled into exactly *twelve over-large jigsaw pieces!* And each of them contained a mosaic picture of each of the creatures that Alice was searching for. Miss Computermite was depicted, as was Captain Ramshackle and the snakely Under Assistant they had met in the knot garden and the chicken-thing they had found in James Marshall Hentrails's automated stomach. These last two floor-pieces were painted over with vicious black crosses. ("I wonder what those black crosses mean?" wondered Alice.) Also pictured on the floor were the zebraman who had helped Whippoorwill across the busy road, and the trumpeting snailman called Long Distance Davis. The next four pieces showed Whiskers Macduff the catgirl, the fishman they had found dead in the librarinth, Professor Chrowdingler and Quentin Tarantula the spiderboy whose *tinier* piece they were currently searching for. All four of these last floor-pieces were marked with the sinister black cross.

"I surmise," echoed and logicuted Celia, "that the black crosses mean that the victim has already been murdered. This is why the serpents call this room THE PRUNING DEPARTMENT."

"But that means that Pablo Ogden's Automated Guitarplayer has been jigsawed!" echoed Alice.

"That's correct. And Pablo is going to be ever so angry about *that*."

"But the Under Assistant snake's picture is also blackcrossed: why should the Civil Serpents want to jigsaw murder one of their own kind?"

"Perhaps he was a traitor to the cause?" echoed Celia. "Perhaps the Under Assistant had decided the means of murder did not justify the end?"

(Once upon a writing time I had considered describing to the reader exactly what the jigsawed body of a snake would look like, but picturing that victim's transformed body became quite a problem to me. I mean to say, how can you possibly jigsaw a snake? There aren't enough *bits* on it to move around. I suppose you could put the head where the tail was, and the tail where the head was, but surely that would only make a snake pointing in the opposite direction! In the end I gave up; the reader must imagine it alone.)

Alice was busily scanning the floor for the last two pieces. "Look, Celia!" she cried. "There's a rendition of Whippoorwill himself! The Civil Serpents want to jigsaw murder Great Aunt Ermintrude's parrot! I *simply* cannot allow that to happen! But I wonder where the twelfth jigsaw piece can be lying?"

"I think we must be *standing* on the twelfth and final piece," Celia suggested. Alice and Celia then looked downwards to find out whose image they were standing on . . .

But there was only a *hole* beneath them! A certain omittance of floor!

Oh no! It's THE PLUMMETING DE . . .

PART . . .

MENT!

Alice screamed out Celia's name as they fell into the yawning gulf of an ellipsis in the marble . . .

"Ce . . .   li . . .

                    a . . .   !   !

                                        !

                                                            "

Alice landed (with a soft plump!) upon a gigantic bed of mattresses. "This is quite the softest thing I've ever landed upon in all of my adventures!" Alice observed to herself, as she bounced up and down. She was so comfortable with her new world, until she realised exactly where she was . . .

Snakes alive!

Alice was in the cellar of the Town Hall, and her soft bed of mattresses was really a vast seething ocean of serpents, who were continuously unknotting and reknotting themselves into new configurations. Alice hopped from one foot to the other, trying to keep her balance!

The cellar stretched out for miles and miles and miles, and the serpents filled every single inch of every single mile. Alice had heard of sea-serpents before, but never had she heard of a sea of serpents: and now here she was actually afloat upon such a thing! Far above her Alice could see the tiny jigsaw-shaped hole in the ceiling through which she and Celia had fallen. Celia was nowhere at all to be seen, but Alice didn't even have time to call out her Automated Sister's name, because just then, the snaking floor beneath her started to move!

Suddenly Alice was riding along on top of the twisting mass of Civil Serpents! Alice was a serpent-surfer! Eventually, she was carried towards the very centre of the cellar, where the gigantic head of a hideously malformed snake thrust its way upwards from the wriggling maelstrom. This monstrous reptile had glistening black slits for eyes; its long snout ended in a pair of jaw-like doors which slowly hinged open to let slip a

dangling rope of thick saliva; two spears it had for fangs, sharp and to the point.

"Good afternoon. My name is Alice," said Alice, curtseying, and crossing her fingers. "Are you the Supreme Serpent?"

The snake flickered out an unrolling red carpet of a forked tongue. This bifurcated implement changed *Alice* into an *Alish*, in a splash of sibilant hissingnesses. "Alish, we meet at lasht!" the serpent sprayed, and then spittled and spattled out this rain of rhymes:

> *"Alish, can you enwonda*
> *About thish Anaconda?*
> *Alish, can you ennoblra*
> *Thish hoodifided Cobra?*
>
> *And can thish girl enshcriptor*
> *This corsheting Conshtrictor?*
> *And can thish girl enladder*
> *The shumming of thish Adder?"*

"Well I'm trying to enladder your meaning, Mrs Big Snake," Alice answered, "but you seem to be rather unsure of which kind of snake you are!" To which the bloated serpent replied with one final hissing verse:

> *"My Alish, can you engrashp*
> *The venom of thish Ashp?*
> *Or even the thirdly Boa*
> *Shmuggled aboard with Noah?"*

"According to my lessons," stated Alice, "there were only a *pair* of boas allowed aboard the Ark. Are you saying that a third boa snake crept into Noah's cargo?"

"That extra sherpent eshcaped from the Garden of Eden," answered the Supreme Snake, "and from there he shlithered aboard the Ark. It was Shatan himshelf in shcaly dishguishe."

"Satan was a stowaway on Noah's Ark?" Alice shuddered.

"Shatan shurvived the flood of your little god by hiding in the water closhet of the Ark. Forty daysh and forty nightsh of torture did he shuffer until he could eshcape to plague mankind onsh more. Shatan Sherpent rulesh Shupreme!"

But Alice wasn't listening. "Why do you keep putting an H after every S?" she complained. "I'm getting covered in your spittle!" (She wouldn't usually have been so impolite, but the shower of snakely saliva was actually burning her skin!)

"It'sh a shpeech impediment I have," replied the serpent with an angry flick of her tongue, before continuing with her story. "We Shivil Sherpentsh are the children of that illishit cargo. *We* are the mosht Shupreme Sherpent!"

"I thought Mrs Minus was trying to *become* the Supreme Serpent?"

"You don't become the Shupreme Sherpent; you become a mere *coil* of the Shupreme Sherpent. We shnakes are the leadersh. There ish only one sherpent. We are Leviathan! We are the World Shnake! The Bashilishk!"

By this time Alice was more or less smothered in snake juice and her skin was very nearly aflame! But this discomfort didn't stop her noticing the small piece of jagged wood impaled upon the serpent's left fang. "That must be the spider piece from my jigsaw!" Alice said to herself, "but how can I possibly steal it back? I doubt if even the Lord's Prayer would work this time, for what single poem could possibly put such a fearsome snake to sleep?"

"Little Alish . . ." the serpent said with a lishp and an ellipshish, "I have an all-sheeing eye. I have followed your progresh through thish tale. I have sheen you hunting down eash piesh of the jigshaw. I have sheen you uncovering evidensh of my mishtakes with the Newmonia fever. I wash only trying to make thish world a better world! You musht have realished how absholutely *random* shoshiety wash becoming? I only wanted the people to conform to the rulesh! Ish that shuch a crime? Sho I fed the Newmonia germ to them all, hoping to make followersh out of them all. Ish it my fault that the exshperiment went wrong? And can you blame myself and my Contortium, Alish, for trying to cover it up with the Jigshaw Murdersh?"

"Yes, I can blame you," answered Alice. "I blame you for *everything!*"

At this accusation, the Supreme Serpent snapped her jaws down and all around Alice. Alice was gathered up into the giant mouth; the twin spears were pricking into her skin! Alice (in her final moments) managed to wriggle free the spidery jigsaw piece from the left-hand fang. And *then* she was swallowed whole!

OOO

Down, down and down! Along, along and along! Around, around and around! Alice had no idea that the insides of a snake could have so many twistings and turnings. Being swallowed was making her quite dizzy, but this didn't stop her from carefully adding the spider's jigsaw piece to the other nine in her pinafore pocket. "What a strange coincidence!" she said to herself whilst being further ingested, "only a few hours ago I swallowed a wurm: and now I'm being swallowed by a snake! The future is filled with writhing!"

Eventually Alice was deposited into a small, dark chamber which contained only a neat and tidy desk: behind the desk sat a neat and tidy man with a neat and tidy fountain-pen in his hand; he was scribbling away at a neat and tidy ledger. "Your name, please?" he neated and tidied.

"Alice."

The neat and tidy man scribbled Alice's name into the ledger, without even looking at her. "Your purpose in the city of Munchester?" he asked.

"To find a way out," answered Alice, which made the neat and tidy man look up at last.

"A way out?" he spluttered. "There is no way out! This is *Munch*ester! The place where food goes after being swallowed."

"What is your name, neat and tidy man?" asked Alice.

"My name *is* Neathan Tidyman; what of it?"

"I want to get back to Manchester, Neathan."

"*Man*chester? Have you your tickling ticket?"

"Oh what a coincidence, Mister Tidyman!" said Alice, remembering Zenith O'Clock's promise. "I have just such a tickling ticket!" Alice pulled Whippoorwill's green-and-yellow feather from her pinafore pocket.

"Ooh, a green-and-yellow feather!" cried Neathan, snatching it from Alice's hand. "I've always wanted a green-and-yellow tickling feather! I can visit the Chimera!" He then proceeded to tickle Alice's nose with it! And then his own! "Oh yes!" he squealed, completely *untidying* himself. "Oh yes! Oh take me!"

Alice saw that three closed doors were waiting beyond the desk. Each had its own little hand-written sign: the first door

read THE THIRD DOOR IS THE SAFE DOOR; the second read THE
FIRST DOOR IS LYING; the third read THE SECOND DOOR IS REALLY
THE FIRST DOOR. "Young girl, choose your door wisely!"
Tidyman giggled as he tickled, "one of them leads to
Munchester; another leads to Unchester; a further one of
them leads to Manchester, and that's the only safe door: the
other two are deadly."

"But which door should I choose?" asked Alice of herself.
"Oh, if only the Automated Alice was still with me! Celia would
quite logically work out the problem. But as Celia isn't with
me, I shall have to pretend to be her. Now then, let me consider . . ." Alice then logicuted thus: "The first door claims the
third door to be the safe door, but the second door claims that
the first door is lying, so maybe the second door is the safe
door. But then the third door says that the second door is really the first door, so it's the second door that is lying, which
means that the first door is telling the truth: therefore the
third door must be the *safe* door . . ."

"Quickly, Alice!" laughed Tidyman. "It's make your mind up
time!"

Alice opened up the third door and walked through it.

DOROTHY,

DOROTHY AND

DOROTHY

THE third door shivered and vanished as soon as Alice stepped through it: now she was standing on a small hill which overlooked a most pleasant landscape. The sun was greeting her with a cheery smile on its bright face. There was a winding country lane that stretched lazily into the haze of summer. A bluebird softly whistled a lovely melody from a nearby willowing tree, and a pair of rabbits in courtship gambolled happily through a field of buttercups. "I must surely have chosen the correct door," Alice congratulated herself, "for this is a very pretty land indeed! If only Celia were here to enjoy this particular part of Manchester with me!"

This was a world where it never could rain, and in the warm and shimmering distance a languid curl of smoke was rising from the chimney of a little wooden cottage. Alice set off down the hill and along the lane towards the cottage, and as she went along the bluebirds and the rabbits called out to her from the hedgerows. "Dear little Alice," they twittered, "how nice of you to visit us!" Alice was quite taken aback by this tenderness, so much so that she completely forgot all about the time and the jigsaw and the murders and even the writing lesson! Her worries were like mists dispersing. Alice walked along without a single care in the whole world, until she came eventually to the small rose-enshrouded cottage. There was a beautifully engraved name-plate on the door, which read DONE WONDERING.

Alice gently tapped her knuckles upon the door, and from within, in answer, came a kindly voice saying, "Come in. It's open."

Alice pushed open the cottage door and stepped inside.

An old, old man was sitting at a dining table, on which two plates of hot roast beef, carrots and potatoes were gently steaming. The smell of food reminded Alice that she hadn't eaten in a long, long time (except for a little wurm, that is!). "You must be hungry, Alice," the man said, gesturing to the second plate, "won't you join me?"

"Thank you, kind sir," said Alice as she sat down.

The old man looked at Alice then. He explored her keenly, as though to remember her forever: but the young girl was so busily feeding her face with the roast beef that she never noticed his eager study. "Have you forgotten me so easily, Alice?" the old man finally found the courage to enquire.

This question caused Alice to pause for a second (with a forkful of boiled carrot halfway to her lips), and to look across the table at the old man. What she saw then made her lower her knife and fork to the plate. "Mister Dodgson!" she cried, and she excused herself from the table and ran all the way around it until she was hugging and snuggling the old man. "You look dreadfully old, kind sir," she whispered to him, "and are those tears in your eyes?"

"And is this beef gravy dribbling from your mouth?" the old man answered.

"But what are you doing in Manchester, Mister Dodgson?"

"This isn't Manchester, Alice; you chose the third door, which was the wrong door."

"But I solved the problem so logically! How could I be wrong?"

"You forget to remember that the second door was really the first door, and therefore the third door was *really* the second door."

"So it was the *second* door I should have taken?"

"That is correct, dear Alice," answered the old man, with a further tear. "The second door would have led you to safety, whereas the third door has led you only to Unchester. This world is where the living come to live after they have finished off living. This is where I live now, having finished my living in the year 1898."

"Oh Mister Dodgson!" cried Alice, "does this mean that I have also died?"

"You were swallowed by the Supreme Serpent, Alice, in the third of my books about you. I tried my best to save you, but I was too old and too tired to rescue you. I'm afraid that this *does* mean that you have died."

"And has dear Celia also been swallowed?" asked Alice.

"Luckily, I managed to allow Celia an escape. I found that her superior automated powers enabled her to resist the serpent's maw."

"But where is Celia now?"

"Would you like some treacle pudding, Alice?" asked the old man.

"1 haven't got time for your trequel pudding!" cried Alice (rather too rudely, I think). "I want my twin twister back! And I want to go home!"

"But that's vurtually impossible, Alice. What's gone is gone . . ."

"But if a thing is only *virtually* impossible, doesn't that mean that it just might be possible?"

"I didn't say virtually: I said vurtually, with a U in the word, instead of an I."

"But I want to escape, unlike *you*, Mister Dodgson."

"Well let me see," considered the old man; "I was a *real* person who once upon a time naturally died: but you, Alice, are both a *real* and an *imaginary* character, and how can imagination be killed? Maybe there is a little way yet for your story to continue . . . although it would mean going against all the rules of life, death and narrative." The Reverend's tears fell like puddles onto his unfinished roast beef. "I was rather hoping we could spend some time together, Alice," he choked, "but perhaps you must really leave me now . . ." And then the Reverend Dodgson leaned close to Alice's face and said these final words, "Will this young Alice kiss me good-bye?"

Alice kissed him, and the old man's lips were salty with life . . .

O☾O

"Flummoxy Wummoxy!"

"I beg your pardon?" said Alice.

"Wibbily Wobbily!"

"I'm afraid I don't understand."

"Lubberly Jubberly!"

"Who are you?" asked Alice.

"Flippety Floppety!"

"Oh, where am I now?" cried Alice.

"Chimeree Shimmeree!"

"This is the Chimera?"

"Flutterly Utterly!"

"Oh dear!" said Alice, "I seem to have landed inside of a Chimera show. Mister Dodgson must have kissed me here, somehow or other."

"Misterly Dodgily!"

"So you're Flippety Floppety?" Alice asked of the orange and blue rabbit that galumphed all around her. "I saw your name on a Chimera poster, isn't that right, Mister Rabbit?"

"Posterly Mosterly!" guffawed the animated rabbit as he jumped, and clung onto Alice's leg!

"What am I doing here?" cried Alice, as she looked all around for an escape. A soft white light covered the whole emptiness she was trapped inside, and within and around the emptiness danced and laughed a group of teasing children. These children were all laughing gleefully at Alice's attempts to shake off the clinging Flippety Floppety rabbit.

"Alice, you've made it at last!" cried another voice. "I've been waiting simply *ages!*" It was Captain Ramshackle's voice calling to Alice from nowhere at all, until she noticed that amidst the children lurked the adult badger-face that belonged to Captain Ramshackle!

"Captain Ramshackle!" Alice cried, "what are *you* doing here?!"

"A little birdy told me where to find you," answered the badgerman.

"Could that birdy be Whippoorwill the parrot?" asked Alice.

"The very same," replied Ramshackle. "He told me you were

currently playing the flutters at the Palace of Chimera in Rusholme. This matinee show is called 'Flippety Floppety Comes Unstuck'; it's a children's projection, and you, Alice, are this week's guest artiste."

"Questingly Guestingly!" squeaked the rabbit as he climbed further up Alice's body.

"But what is Chimera?" asked Alice of the Captain, "and how can I escape this rather rampant rabbit?"

And the children laughed to see such fun!

"Chimera is like the theatre or a lantern show," Ramshackle replied, "except that it's more *real*. You have to tickle your nose with a tickling feather, and then you actually become a part of the story. You get *turned on* to it. It's called a collected vurtual experience."

"But how can I escape being vurtually collected?" asked Alice with a U.

"It's quite easy," said the badgerman, "you must turn yourself off."

"But how do I turn myself off?"

"Just say the words DONE WONDERING out loud." And as Ramshackle said the words DONE WONDERING out loud he dissolved into the light and disappeared from the Chimera. So Alice immediately followed suit. "DONE WONDERING!" she cried out loud . . .

oCCO

Alice then found herself sitting in a cold, damp seat in the dark beside Captain Ramshackle. In front of them on the vast

wall fluttered the images of Flippety Floppety and the children, and all around her in the rows of seats sat the children
themselves, tickling their pert little noses with a collection of
tickling feathers. The children's eyes were all glazed over like
cup-cakes and filled with wonder-dust. Captain Ramshackle
untickled his own nose and then took Alice's hand, to lead her
towards an illuminated REALITY THIS WAY sign.

Outside, in the grounds of the Rusholme Palace of Chimera,
Pablo Ogden's garden shed was sitting patiently upon the con-
crete. Captain Ramshackle led Alice to the shed's door, relat-
ing upon the way, "After hearing Professor Chrowdingler's tale
of woe, I decided it best to gather together all the remaining-
alive witnesses to the Civil Serpents' murderously jigsawing
plan, in order to best protect them. And here they all are!" At
which he opened up the shed door and pushed Alice inside.

Alice looked around the crowded garden shed, and there indeed they all were! There was Miss Computermite grown to human size; and there was the zebraman (whose name turned out to be Stripey); and there was Long Distance Davis, the snailman, playing a lonesome note upon his trumpet! And there, oh there! was Pablo Ogden, the Reverse Butcher himself, weeping over a pile of rubbish that Alice recognised to be James Marshall Hentrails's jigsawed remains. "How dare they rearrange my finest creation so?" Pablo was wailing. "Those silly serpents will pay for this undoing!"

Celia, the Automated Alice, however, was not there: but Alice didn't even have a second to think about that, because straightaway Stripey the zebraman was shouting out (in a black-and-white voice), "Pablo, the police are approaching at a rate of knots on the starboard bow!"

"And they're in their whirlybird!" added Ramshackle.

"It's not the police," squeaked Miss Computermite, "it's Mrs Minus!" (At which news, Long Distance Davis immediately vanished into the shell of his hat, which at least made a little more room in the shed!)

"All hands on deck!" shouted Pablo, and Alice really did think she was on a *ship* for a moment, especially when Pablo started to pull upon the series of levers which lifted the garden shed onto its rickety-chickeny legs. "Our destination, Alice?" he called out, taking over the wheel.

"To my Great Aunt Ermintrude's home in Didsbury!" replied Alice.

"I'm not sure if I know the way," said Pablo.

"Oh dear," said Alice, "neither do I."

"If I may make a logical suggestion," said Miss Computermite, "perhaps we should follow that green-and-yellow parrot; *he* seems to know the way."

"Full steam ahead!" bellowed Pablo and off the shed lurched at a frightening pace, along the road.

"Whippoorwill!" cried Alice, and rushed to the shed's front window to watch the parrot's colourfully flashing flight. "What time is it, Captain Ramshackle?" she asked (whilst hardly daring to ask!). The badgerman consulted his wrist-clock: "It's just gone almost exactly, not quite nearly, half-past one."

"Thirty minutes left!" worked out Alice. "I do hope we get there in time!"

But they were making a tremendous pace by now: the garden shed had already carried them along Oxford Road. (You should have seen how it *leapt* over the houses!) Now it was transporting them down Wilmslow Road towards Didsbury; and what a marvellous transport a walking, running, hopping, skipping and jumping garden shed can make: how easily it can scamper over the driving droves of auto-horses! Miss Computermite had climbed out of the window (quite an easy task when you have *six* legs!): she was now perched on the shed's roof, shouting out directions from there, and keeping her eyes on stalks for the flutterings of the distant parrot. Stripey the zebraman was stationed at the back window of the shed: his job was to keep a lookout for Mrs Minus's automated whirlybird. ("She's catching up with us, Pablo!" was Stripey's incessant cry. "Faster! Faster!") Pablo was at the steering wheel, trying his best to urge the shed forwards. Long Distance Davis was still firmly curled into his shell-hat (which was rolling around the shed's floor like a corkscrewed bowling ball, and threatening at any minute to fall out!). Alice was trying her best to be useful, but Captain Ramshackle wasn't trying to be useful at all! Instead he was dancing around excitedly whilst chanting out yet another verse of his little song:

> *"Oh garden sheds may play the fool*
> *Upon the snakes of big;*
> *But all I want's the crooked rule*
> *That makes a jigsaw jig."*

But somehow or other the six strange travellers managed to stay on board and to work together in a rather slipshod ship-shape fashion. (Or should I say a slipshod shedshape fashion?) Whatever, shipshape *or* shedshape, the intrepid half-a-dozen made a pretty pace. Through Rusholme they rushed home; through Fallowfield they ploughed a fallow and through Withington they (almost) withered: until, finally, Didsbury and its sprawling cemetery were in their sights. The place where Manchester buried its dead. Alice looked down from the garden shed's tottering heights, as she tried to locate her Great Aunt's house. The cemetery looked a lot *sprawlier* than Alice remembered it, but she supposed to herself (correctly of course) that many many more people must have died since she was last here in 1860. Now she spotted Whippoorwill landing on the broken-down roof of an old, decrepit house. "That can't be right!" said Alice. "Great Aunt Ermintrude would *never* let her house get into such an untidy state!" But the house certainly seemed to be in the right place, as far as Alice could remember: it was just that the cemetery had grown so much in the intervening years, that it had actually *grown* all around the old house!

"Put me down here, Pablo!" Alice said to the shed's pilot.

"I don't think I've got any choice," answered Pablo.

"What do you mean?" asked Alice.

"Whirlybird gaining on the stern, Pablo!" shouted Stripey the zebraman. "Her cannon is loaded!"

"I think we're about to be fired at!" cried Pablo. "Nobody panic!"

But of course, everybody aboard did panic, especially when they heard the cannon-ball *whizzing* through the air towards them! The cannon-ball hit the left leg of the shed! The leg crumpled up like a roasted chicken leg that has been kept too long in the oven, and then the whole *world* keeled over to one side and crashed to the ground!

Everybody tumbled out of the fallen shed into the grave-yard. The garden shed was splintered into a thousand pieces and Pablo Ogden was shaking an angry fist at the hovering whirlybird. "How dare you!" he cursed at Mrs Minus, who was gazing down calmly from the safety of the whirlybird; the snakewoman was smiling at him with her evil little fangs. "I'll get you for this destruction!" Pablo shouted.

"I don't care for *you*," responded Mrs Minus. "It's Alice I want."

But Alice didn't want to be wanted by Mrs Minus; all that Alice wanted was to reach the house of her Great Aunt in time for her journey to the past. All around her were jutting gravestones and sculptured angels. The old house was lying in the midst of all these memorials and it looked as dead as a doornail. Why, even the doornails in its rotting door looked as dead as doornails!

Alice looked around quickly to see that all of her fellow shed-travellers were alive and well. Miss Computermite had reduced herself to her former size in order to scurry into the nearest crevice; Long Distance Davis had become a shiny snail slithering along a gravestone's edge; Stripey the zebraman had turned into a mere play of shadow and light amongst the tombs; Captain Ramshackle was already burrowing a deep sett into the cemetery's soil. Pablo Ogden was still cursing at Mrs Minus on the whirlybird as it lowered itself to the ground.

All amongst the gravestones the policedogmen were gathering in their packs, but they were keeping their distance, and Alice couldn't work out why. Inspector Jack Russell stepped forward from the pack of dogs, but he merely looked at Alice along the sights of his long snout; he didn't even *try* to arrest her. Alice was puzzled by this uncommon behaviour, but then she heard Whippoorwill squawking from the garden of the house, and Alice rushed forwards to greet him. It wasn't really a garden of course, it was just an extension of the cemetery. The parrot was perched upon a crumbling gravestone set directly in front of the house. Alice expected Whippoorwill to deliver yet another riddle, but no such thing happened. Alice

ERMINTRUDE
AND
MORTIMER
PEABODY

NOT DEAD,

saw that he had a little something lodged in his beak, which forbade him to make even a single squawk.

It was a jigsaw piece. Alice realised that this jigsaw piece was Whippoorwill's last and final riddle. She pulled it loose, and saw that it was a crooked picture of a blur of green-and-yellow feathers. Alice added it deftly to the others in her pinafore pocket, and it was only then that she noticed the names engraved upon the gravestone that Whippoorwill was perched upon:

ERMINTRUDE AND MORTIMER PEABODY

NOT DEAD, ONLY RADISHING

Indeed, there was a rash of radishes growing all around the grave. Alice suddenly remembered Professor Chrowdingler's ruling that she had to eat some radishes *backwards* in order to return to the past. But how *do* you eat a radish backwards? Alice pulled up a knotted specimen by the leaves, and then bent double in order to thrust her face through her legs, backwards: and then she bit into the root. Naughty Whippoorwill, when offered some radish, mimicked her to do the same. Alice laughed, to see such a backwards parrot!

If Alice was suddenly expecting to be transported back to 1860, she was to be bitterly disappointed. "Oh Whippoorwill!" she exclaimed, "the chrownons in this radish haven't worked! I fear that we're trapped in the future forever!"

But then the door to the old house opened up with a creaking sigh, and Celia the Automated Alice stepped onto the porch. "Fear not, my little sister," stated the doll, calmly, "we are almost home." Celia was looking so much like Alice by this time, that Alice really did think she was seeing herself walk towards herself!

"Celia!" cried Alice, "so you managed to reach our Great Aunt's house before me? And you managed to escape the snakes!"

"Not quite yet," answered Celia, "for isn't that Mrs Minus creeping through the gravestones towards us, with her fangs glinting in the sun?"

Alice looked over her shoulder: there indeed was the evil Civil Serpent, and her fangs *were* glinting! "But why aren't Inspector Jack Russell and the other policedogmen trying to help Mrs Minus arrest me?" asked Alice.

"Professor Chrowdingler had posted her evidence of the serpent's Newmonia crime to the police yesterday," said Celia, "and the Inspector received that evidence a mere thirty minutes ago."

"So the police are now on our side?"

"It would seem so."

"So why won't they arrest Mrs Minus?"

"The police are scared of her."

Alice looked around at the approaching shape of Mrs Minus. The snakewoman had become even more of a snake than a woman, and she had drawn out an evil-looking pistol. "Well I'm scared of her as well!" said Alice. "So am I!" squawked Whippoorwill, as he fluttered into the house.

"And so am I!" copied Celia. "Alice, come into the house quickly!"

It started to rain again (and quite viciously this time, with some streaks of lightning!), as Alice ran into the antique house after her sister.

Once inside the house, they locked the front door behind them and ran towards the breakfast room from which Alice had long ago vanished. There, still, was the ancient grandfather clock and the empty birdcage, and there still, the uncompleted jigsaw puzzle upon the breakfast table. Nothing had changed except for the thick dust which settled in waves over the decaying furniture. The rain was still lashing against the window, and the cemetery was still brooding in the downpour, and the lightning was still flashing. The clock was *tick-tocking* away at five minutes to two (even though it was now covered in horrible cobwebs).

Alice quickly removed the eleven jigsaw pieces from her pinafore pocket, then proceeded to slot them into place in the mouldy old jigsaw puzzle of London Zoo: the termite into the Insect House; the badger in the Badger House; the snake in the Reptile House; the chicken into the Hen House; the zebra into the Mammal House; the snail into the Gastropod House; the cat into the Feline House; the fish into the Aquarium; the crow into the Aviary; the spider into the Arachnid House; the parrot also into the Aviary. At the adding of that piece, Whippoorwill fluttered back into his cage. Eleven creatures were now feeling quite at home, but still the twelfth jigsaw piece was missing.

"Oh where can that final elusive piece be?" Alice cried whilst searching all over the room for it. "It must be here somewhere! Help me find it, Celia!"

Celia had her head stuck in the clock's case, saying, "I'm doing my best, Alice." Then she popped back out: "But all I've found up to now is this." She was clutching the very first feather that Whippoorwill had dropped in his flight to the future.

"That's no use," replied Alice. "Quickly! Keep searching."

"Four minutes to two, Alice," whispered the clock.

"Oh dear!" cried Alice. "The jigsaw piece must be somewhere! Perhaps it's fallen down the sofa cushions?" Imagine her surprise, to find that three identical old and wizened women were sitting on the sofa! So covered in dust and cobwebs they were, and so ancient and withered, that Alice had thought them merely part of the furniture until then! "And who are you *three?*" she demanded.

"We are the tripletted daughters of Ermintrude . . ." they answered all of a piece.

"My name is Dorothy . . ." the first woman said.

"My name also is Dorothy . . ." the second added.

"My name also and also is Dorothy . . ." completed the third.

"So you're the answer to my two o'clock writing lesson!" said Alice. "You three are the Dot and the Dot and the Dot of an ellipsis!"

"That is correct . . ." answered the three Dots all together. "We are the Ellipsisters . . . and you must be Alice . . ." But they were talking to Celia!

"*I'm* Alice!" corrected Alice. "*That* is Celia."

"We didn't realise you had a twin sister, Alice . . ." the three women said.

"And I didn't realise that you three Dorothys would still be here," replied Alice. "Why have you let this house get into such a state?"

"Time slowed to a standstill for us since you vanished, Alice . . . We never married, you know . . ."

"Three minutes to two, Alice," whispered the clock and then there was a sudden, furious banging on the front door!

"Oh no!" screamed Alice.

"It's Mrs Minus trying to get in!" added Celia.

It was all too much for Alice: "I'll never find the final jigsaw piece now!" she snuffled.

"But dear Alice," the three Dorothys tripletted in tandem, "*you* are the final jigsaw piece . . ."

"But that's impossible!" Alice sobbed. "I'm a girl, not a piece in a puzzle!"

"I think they might be right, Alice," said Celia.

Alice ran to the breakfast table. There was the dusty old jigsaw picture with its little crooked hole where the last piece was missing. Alice saw that the hole wasn't actually *inside* one of the various animal cages: it was actually a hole in the pathways *between* the cages, the pathways where the visitors could wander. In fact the hole was missing from a young girl's head! And the girl had on a red pinafore! "Well I suppose that might be me," said Alice, "but I would never fit in such a *tiny* opening! Especially with Celia!"

"I'm not coming with you, Alice," said Celia.

"Of course you're coming with me!" said Alice.

"I'm afraid I didn't eat the radishes, Alice. But the truth

is . . . I rather like living in the future." Celia stuck Whippoorwill's lost feather in her hair, as she said this. "The future is my proper home."

"Celia!" cried Alice, as the clock whispered, "Two minutes to two, Alice!"

"Alice!" shouted Mrs Minus as she whipped her scaly tail at the front door of the house. Everything was happening all at once!

Celia suddenly said to Alice, "Shall we open the cupboard in my left-hand-side thigh?"

"The one TO BE OPENED IN AN *EXTREME* EMERGENCY ONLY?"

"That's the one, Alice."

So Alice opened up the tiny door in Celia's thigh: inside, she found only a small lead ball labelled with the words SHOOT ME. "Shoot me from what?" asked Alice. At which question, Celia unbuttoned her pinafore.

"One minute to two, Alice!" *tick-tocked* the clock, gaining a frightful pace!

The front door was being smashed down into firewood! "Mrs Minus has broken through!" cried Alice.

"Stay calm, my sister. Open me up, please." Celia had revealed her bare, porcelain stomach, in the middle of which nestled another small door. Alice opened this cupboard; a flintlock pistol was lodged within Celia's inner workings. FIRE ME said its label.

"I can't use *that*," said Alice.

"Pablo Ogden has built this gun into my body for a purpose," answered Celia. "Hand me the shot."

Alice gave the lead ball to Celia. Just then, Mrs Minus burst into the breakfast room! She had by now turned more or less fully into a giant snake! Only a single human hand extended from her reptilian body, and within its grip rested her own pistol. Mrs Minus aimed the pistol directly at Alice's heart. "You will pay for your treachery, my young girl!" she hissed, whilst beginning to squeeze on the trigger.

Time became stilled for a single second.

And then, how the snakewoman screamed! Alice saw that a certain invisible but sharply clawed cat had pounced upon Mrs Minus.

"My sweet Quark!" Alice whispered, "you have come to save me!" But Mrs Minus threw off the invisible cat, and raised her gun once again.

"It's two o'clock, Alice!" whispered the grandfather clock, "time to go home!" And then it donged a first ding!

And by that first ding, Celia had managed to load her own pistol.

Mrs Minus squeezed her trigger, but—

Celia squeezed hers first!

Mrs Minus was splatter-snaked all over the walls!

Alice climbed onto the dining table, and jumped down into the remaining jigsaw hole . . .

And in the time it takes to turn over the page of a book . . .

WHAT TIME
DO YOU CALL THIS,
ALICE?

...THE

clock dinged its second dong, and Alice landed with a soft *flump!* into her armchair, and then she awoke with a sudden start.

"Oh what a curious dream!" Alice said to herself. "Why, it was almost *real*!" She rubbed at her eyes and then looked at the grandfather clock in the corner; it was, more or less, exactly two o'clock. "I must have fallen asleep in the armchair!" Alice got up and moved to the window; the rain was lashing against the glass and the lightning was flashing over the gravestones in the cemetery.

"Squawk, squawk!" screeched Whippoorwill from his cage.

Suddenly, the dining room door was flung open! "What time do you call this, Alice?" bellowed Great Aunt Ermintrude from the doorway.

"I call it the past time," answered Alice (without really knowing why).

"A pastime!" screamed her Great Aunt. "Do you really think that life is a game, Alice? Well, let me tell you: life is a lesson to be hard-earned! I don't suppose you've finished your *latest* lesson, about the correct usage of an ellipsis?"

"An ellipsis, Great Aunt Ermintrude," began Alice quite confidently, "is a series of three dots at the end of an unfinished sentence, which implies a certain omittance of words, a certain lingering doubt . . ."

"Very good, Alice!" responded Great Aunt Ermintrude (with surprise), "but I'm afraid there's no such word as omittance. There's an admittance, or else there's an omission, but there's no such word between the two! We have a *great deal of work* yet to do on your grammar!" Ermintrude then walked over to the breakfast table. "I see that you've finished your jigsaw of London Zoo. So you managed to find the missing pieces . . . ?"

"Yes, I managed it," answered Alice, quietly.

"Oh my goodness! There's a hideous white ant crawling over the jigsaw . . ."

"It's not an ant, Great Aunt," Alice tried to say, "it's a termite."

"I don't care if it's a prize peacock! I won't allow such vermin in my house!" And before Alice could do anything at all, her Great Aunt had cruelly *squashed* the creature under her fingers! "And where is the new doll that I bought you?" her Great Aunt then asked.

"She is lost, Great Aunt."

"You *mean to say* that you don't know where the doll is?"

"Oh, I know where she is, Great Aunt."

"May I suggest then, Alice, that you retrieve her?"

"Oh I will, Great Aunt," said Alice in a mutter, "one of these days . . ."

"Stop muttering, you naughty little girl!" screeched Ermintrude. "It's very rude! Now it's time for *today's* writing lesson. Pencils out! Books open! Today we shall learn all about the differences between the past and the present tenses."

"I know all about *those* differences!" Alice said (strictly to herself, of course!).

OOO

And thus began the next lesson, and the next one after that, and then the next one after that: all the lessons of life that Alice had to learn, both in Manchester and then in the South of England upon her return, and then throughout the rest of her long life. Alice came to realise that the whole of life could be one long continuous hard lesson. (If you weren't careful, that is!) But Alice had also come to realise that life could be a continuous dream, and as Alice got older and older and older, she never forgot to let a little soft dream into her hard lessons. During the more miserable of her moods, she would find herself revisiting the memories of her three journeys into dreamland: the *wonder* of life, the *mirror* of life, the *future* of life.

This story should rightfully end upon this very moment.

But I must add that (just *occasionally*) Alice would feel a terrible itching feeling inside her skull. Why, it was just as though a thousand termites were running hither and thither with tickling messages! And sometimes (just *sometimes*) Alice would feel a certain stiffness in her limbs, as though her legs and arms were not quite fleshy enough. Often she would find her limbs doing things that she had not quite willed them to do! At those moments Alice really did think that her limbs had a life of their own, as though her limbs were automated appendages.

"Perhaps, in the turmoil of those last moments in the future," Alice would sometimes whisper to herself, "I was confused with Celia? Perhaps it was the Automated Alice that really came back to the past?"

And until the very end of her God-given days, my dear, sweet Alice was unable to decide for certain if she was really real, or else really imaginary . . .

Which do *you* think she was?

All along the stream of time and tears
Under skies where sunlight fades to breath,
Through hours and minutes, weeks and years,
Onwards gliding, we moor at last in death.

My name is like the sun in apogee,
Ascending only to wane and wax the moon.
To all who read this rhyme of apology;
Excuse this waning of Carroll by Noon.

Dodo Dodgson, long since died, transported
Alice to the realms of tale and feather.
Life is but a dream that time has courted;
In dreamings a girl could live forever.

Conclude this tale, my Alice in Auto;
Emerge to life an Alice immortal.

A B O U T   T H E   A U T H O R

JEFF NOON is also a musician, a painter, and a playwright. He was born on the outskirts of Manchester, England, where he still lives today. He is the author of *Vurt*, which won the 1994 Arthur C. Clarke Award, and *Pollen*. He is the recipient of the 1995 John W. Campbell Award for best new writer.